"Leave that man be," the captain said.

Captain Sharps rose from where he had fallen under Hopkins's blow and strode over to where the master-at-arms was preparing to haul the unconscious man below. He stepped up to the stricken Hopkins, seized him by the throat, and dragged him to his feet. Then he walked Hopkins back to the stern rail.

"Look away aft," Captain Sharps commanded. "Tell me what you see. Speak!"

"A ship," Hopkins said. His voice creaked like a door hinge gone cracked and rusty from disuse.

"Look again," the captain said. "What do you see?"

"Death." His voice was now closer to a shriek.

"Yes," Captain Sharps said. "Death pursues us. We have come all this distance to fight death."

LAND OF MIST AND SNOW

DEBRA DOYLE
AND JAMES D. MACDONALD

An Imprint of HarperCollins*Publishers*

EOS
An Imprint of HarperCollins*Publishers*
10 East 53rd Street
New York, New York 10022-5299

Copyright © 2006 by James D. Macdonald and Debra Doyle
ISBN-13: 978-0-06-081919-4
ISBN-10: 0-06-081919-7
www.eosbooks.com

First Eos paperback printing: December 2006

HarperCollins® and Eos® are trademarks of HarperCollins Publishers Inc.

Printed in the U. S. A.

10 9 8 7 6 5 4 3 2 1

IN MEMORIAM
LARRY L. DOYLE
MARGARET ESTERL MACDONALD

LAND OF MIST AND SNOW

The narrative of Lieutenant John Nevis, USN.

IN LATE JANUARY OF 1863 I WAS AN IDLER, AS-
signed to the War Department office at 88 Whitehall
Street in the city of New York after my ship, USS
Tisdale, burned when the Rebels took Norfolk.

Time weighed heavily upon me. The war, which
some had at first expected to be over in a matter of
weeks—or a few months at most—would soon be
entering its third year, and I could not fail to perceive that matters stood at a most perilous juncture.
In the west, the free movement of our forces up and
down the Mississippi still broke upon the rock that
was Confederate-held Vicksburg; to the east and
south, in the Atlantic and the Gulf of Mexico, Rebel
commerce raiders and blockade runners ranged
freely. Everywhere, my brother officers were gaining rank and experiencing sea-time, whether in
gunboats on the inland waterways or in warships
on the open seas, maintaining the blockade and
chasing Confederate raiders.

Meanwhile, I sat filing papers in an obscure office.

President Lincoln had freed all the slaves in Rebel territory. My daily hope was that some similar edict would arrive to free me from my own labors. From my window overlooking the harbor, I could watch the Navy's vessels come and go—a species of keen torture, since I feared that such a long period of shore duty would see my career stalled, if not derailed entirely, the ultimate goal of command at sea forever placed beyond my reach.

So it was that on the morning of January 31st a messenger found me laboring at my desk, checking one long bureaucratic list against another. He had an envelope from the Navy Department in his hand, with my name on the front. I fairly tore the envelope from his grasp and opened it.

What it contained was indeed the answer to my nightly prayer. I was detached immediately from my current assignment and ordered to travel by fastest available means to the Naval Arsenal at Watervliet. There I was to inspect and take possession of a dozen ten-inch Rodman guns, thence to accompany them to the place where USS *Nicodemus* might lie, in order to take my position as head of her gunnery department. *Nicodemus* was new construction; I would be a plank owner. I was further informed that *Nicodemus* was even then being fitted out in preparation for her sea trials.

The remainder of the morning I spent in checking out of my temporary billet, drawing my health and pay records, and turning over my responsibilities to a hapless civilian clerk.

I had been staying at a hotel under *per diem*. I lost no time in packing, and the afternoon saw me at the Hudson River Railroad station in my dress blue uniform, purchasing a ticket to Albany. It was long past dark by the time a hired carriage deposited me at the gates of the Arsenal.

A Marine guard directed me to the duty officer, who saw to my placement in the bachelor officers' quarters. There I said my prayers and went to sleep, wondering what kind of craft *Nicodemus* might be. I had not heard of her before, though in an eddying backwater such as my office at Whitehall Street that would not be a surprise. Still, a sloop of war mounting a broadside of six Rodmans and, I supposed, lesser pieces besides, would be sufficient. I was well satisfied with my prospects.

Morning found me in the Arsenal commander's office, presenting my compliments and my orders. The commander, a pleasant enough fellow named Winchell who had preceded me by two years at the Academy, greeted me and offered to accompany me himself on my inspection tour of the guns. I felt it was hardly my place to refuse, and I was just as glad to talk again with a sailor; my previous tour had placed me among civilians and invalided Army men, landsmen all.

As it turned out, he wanted to do more than talk of mutual acquaintances while showing off his command to an outsider. He wanted to pump me for information, information that I sadly lacked, and which baffled me as well.

"You see, Johnny," he said as we entered the sheds facing the Hudson where the guns stood, "they're cast to spec, though why the devil the specs were written that way eludes me."

The guns stood in a burnished rank, gleaming the yellow-gold of brass.

"Brass cannon," I said.

"Yes, brass, as ordered," Winchell said, and here he gestured to a petty officer standing by. "And virgin brass too; never before made into any other shape."

The petty officer strode over and presented his leader with a sheaf of paper, which he reviewed, then handed to me. It was the casting history of each of the Rodmans, from the first smelting of the copper and zinc to the present.

I checked over the cannon carefully. I was no stranger to ordnance; the lives of myself and my shipmates, not to mention the defeat of our enemies, were dependent on the flawless construction and operation of the cannon. I requested an inspection mirror and a light, and examined every inch of the barrels, inside and out. They did in fact appear to be without scratch, crack, or other imperfection.

I turned to Winchell at length. "You can be proud of your work, sir," I said.

"Do you wish to examine the ammunition as well?" he inquired.

"To the same specifications?" said I.

"The same, virgin brass."

"I can't believe it will be necessary to handle each

ball," I said, which brought a smile to his lips. Winchell gave orders that the cannon were to be crated and loaded on a barge for transport. He then invited me to join him for a belated lunch. I accepted with pleasure.

Over cigars at the officers' club, I made bold to breach the question directly.

"Where is it that these guns that I just signed for are to be shipped?"

"To Brooklyn, for the Navy Yard. So say the lading documents. They are being loaded onto a barge even now. A steam tug will tow them. Beyond that, I know nothing."

Across the river in Manhattan I had not heard of a ship under construction that required brass cannon. I asked Winchell directly if he had ever heard of such a vessel.

"No, indeed not. But I can scarcely hear of everything. Perhaps she's been laid in Charlestown."

"Perhaps."

He kindly walked me to the barge at quayside where my dozen Rodmans, neatly crated, now lay side by side on a barge. Crates that I supposed contained brass shot filled a second barge. We shook hands, saluted, and I presented my orders to the master of the civilian tug that was to take me down the same river that I had only lately ascended. The pilothouse of the tug was cramped, and the smell of the engines pervasive, but I eagerly accepted the offer to make the journey there.

A brisk wind was blowing, adding its bite to the

winter air, while the sun dipped toward the western hills. A young enlisted man brought my seabag from my quarters on shore and laid it on the fantail of the tug, lashed to the rail. Towing hawsers were made fast to the barges, and with our whistles screaming out we made way down river. The sun set as we steamed along, the lighthouses of the Hudson illuminated, as we made our way to the East River of Manhattan and to the Navy Yard on its eastern shore.

We came alongside a brig, TRIUMPH lettered on her sternboard in gold leaf, where we were evidently expected. The watch soon appeared with a lantern, a ladder dropped to our deck, and a working party swung out booms to load the cargo from the barge to the brig's hold.

I clambered up the ladder, my boat cloak swirling around me, to salute the quarterdeck and the officer of the deck.

The degree of activity surprised me, and I said as much. I had expected the guns to be loaded at first light, no sooner, for the night was a dark and a bitter one.

"Dark and cold, you'll get used to 'em where you're going," the officer said. "We sail with the tide or miss a day, and that won't make the old man happy, not a bit."

He concluded reading my orders by the binnacle lamp, then handed them back to me and instructed the messenger of the watch to take me below and show me to the captain's quarters, then to my own.

The captain, as it turned out, was "Uncle Joe" Suffern, of whom I had heard good report. He was a seaman's seaman, and a fighting captain. Why he was assigned to such a small vessel and such an insignificant role as running coastwise cargo I could not at that time imagine.

"Last of the *Nicodemus* wardroom," he said, having offered me a seat in his cabin and a glass of port. "I envy you. The outfitting should be done soon. I imagine sea trials shortly."

"*Nicodemus*, sir? While my orders assign me to her, I confess that I do not know her."

"You are not aware? You and your guns are being transshipped to the Naval Experimental Shipyard, Thule."

"I've never heard of that shipyard either, sir."

"Neither had I, until I was assigned to run cargo there. Not to breathe a word about the place to anyone, not even to a sweetheart or a wife, those are our instructions."

"I have neither," I said. "But what can you tell me about *Nicodemus*?"

"Nothing," he replied, "for I have not seen her myself, though I have been involved in her construction for over a year now."

Our conversation was interrupted by a messenger who announced the loading complete and the cargo made fast for sea. Captain Suffern excused himself, directed the boy to show me to my cabin, and took to the deck. I followed the messenger toward the waist, where I was to be placed in a cabin shared with another lieutenant. My seabag was already there, lying on the deck beside a stanchion.

I traded my boat cloak for a short jacket of thick wool and ascended the ladder to the main deck. The boatswain piped, *Single up all lines,* and the crew, well drilled, hurried silently to obey.

"Cast off," came a voice from the quarterdeck, and the line-handling party on the pier dropped the mooring lines from the bollards. The same tug that had carried the guns from Watervliet pulled us stern first into the stream, then cast off.

We hoisted sail, and beneath topgallants and the glittering stars we passed beneath the Battery. I could see the War Department building, one window on the top floor illuminated by the lantern of a late worker. I imagined that it might be my relief burning the midnight oil, and raised my hat to him as we passed.

As we entered the Narrows the word was passed to make full sail, and the little brig fairly bounded forward under a fresh breeze. By sunrise we were out of sight of land, the ship's head east by north, shaping a course for who knew where.

From the private diary of Miss Columbia Abrams. (Note: This diary was kept in Miss Abrams's personal shorthand.)

MARCH 4TH, 1863

WHEN I WAS STILL A SCHOOLGIRL WITH MY HAIR IN pigtails, I used to dream of going on adventures. Our teachers warned us, then and later, that we should strive to keep our thoughts from dwelling upon such things, lest the power of our untutored minds should act upon the universe to bring us those dreamed-of gifts which—they assured us—we should not appreciate nearly as much as we expected.

Perhaps I should not have taken their warnings as an encouragement, for today I find myself embarked upon an adventure indeed. Father and I leave Washington today for New York, where I am to board the ship that will take me northward to a secret destination—sworn to the Union and the Constitution as much as any man in the naval service.

I begin this journal, therefore, in a spirit of gratitude toward my younger self, whose persistence in her fantasies of high adventure and deeds of great renown may have borne in the end their wished-for fruit. If so, then it is thanks to her that I have been chosen for the task that is mine to carry out.

While I was a student at the Hadley Female Academy, I dreamed—as did most of my classmates—of playing a part in the great struggle of our time, to preserve the Union and to advance the cause of Abolition. I feared that my contribution would be limited by my gender to the singing of inspirational songs, since my knitting is so bad that only a truly desperate soldier would want socks or a muffler from my hand. But thanks to Mr. Cornelius Vanderbilt and his friend Captain Sharps, I have a place in this venture; indeed, I recall Mr. Vanderbilt saying, when first Captain Sharps put forth his extraordinary proposal, that my father was fortunate to have a daughter so aptly suited for the work.

At the same time, because I have vowed that in these pages I shall write only that which is true, no matter how much dissimulation might be required of me elsewhere, I must admit that I feel a certain amount of apprehension. Not fear—or at least not yet, though I own it could become such—but we live in a time of war, and in such a time, to be aboard a ship in the Union's service is to face the prospect, or rather the certainty, of conflict.

I can only hope that when the hour of battle comes I will comport myself with courage and dignity, as befits a daughter of the Commonwealth of Massachusetts and a graduate of the Hadley Female Academy.

A letter from Mr. Wm. R. Sharps,
Philosophiae Doctor, *to*
Mr. Cornelius Vanderbilt.

BOSTON
30 APRIL 1861

I HAVE STRIVEN, I HAVE PERSISTED, I HAVE EN-
dured, and my efforts have been crowned on this date
with success.

Long I have labored toward this end. By the time the
renegade *filibustero* William Walker escaped the
condign vengeance that you meted out to his confrere
Garrison, and rumor spoke of vows made on his part
to dark and bloody gods, I had already found the
missing pages of the Grey Book.
 Copies of the Grey Book are common enough, as
volumes of arcana go. The text contains enough chants
and invocations to make it a favorite of dabblers, while
the *cognoscenti*, misled by its reputation as an exer-

cise manual for beginners, largely hold it in contempt.
Most of the modern versions are based on the Aldine
Press edition of 1501; Aldus Manutius, for his part,
drew his text from the San Marco manuscript of the
Liber Pallidus, which scholars of his day accepted as
both the most ancient and the most complete.

I was, myself, no metaphysician when I first encountered the text, merely a student of paleography
and epigraphy and textual transmission. My work
with the Grey Book was meant, at the time, to be
nothing more than a research exercise, confirming—
by means of diligent comparison between the various
extant manuscript versions—that Aldus had typeset
the San Marco *Liber Pallidus* as nearly word for word
as possible.

The task demanded close reading, not just of the
Aldine Press edition and the San Marco MS, but of
all the manuscripts of the *Liber Pallidus* known to
be extant at the time of the first printing. I performed
the task to the satisfaction of my instructors (indeed,
I took my degree with highest honors on the basis of
that work), but I kept to myself what else I had determined in the course of my investigations: that the
San Marco MS is a deliberately defective text. There
are no visible excisions; the scriptorium that produced it created an incomplete copy *de novo*.

Comparison with the Regensburg Codex—held
now in a private library in Massachusetts, and long
ignored by scholars on the grounds of being younger
than the San Marco MS, as well as having been un-
available to Aldus working in Venice—bears this

out. Internal evidence indicates that the two manuscripts derive from a common ancestor. In the case of the Regensburg Codex, the missing text was literally excised, the pages cut from the binding with a sharp knife.

In a leap of intuition, I realized that the text missing from the San Marco and Regensburg manuscripts must have contained the rituals and requirements needed to shape the trivial invocations of the Grey Book into tools of great power—power so great that an entire generation of European savants saw fit to neuter their own work rather than let it survive into the age of the printed word.

The realization enraged me: those sages of old had understood that the many copies of a text made by a printer could not be held close and controlled as could a single manuscript; and they had despised the common crowd. Well then, I said to them, or to the shades that I fancied hovered still about the old handwritten texts, here I am, child of the New World and the common man, and I shall find your secrets out.

I became from that moment a man obsessed. My earlier studies meant nothing to me, save as a preparation for the metaphysical disciplines into which I now threw myself. I exhausted the libraries of New York, Arkham, the Vatican, Köln, Liège, and St. Petersburg. What books could teach me, I learned; when I could learn from books no further, I sought living masters to teach me more. Always, wherever I went and with whomever I studied, I kept in mind the missing pages of the *Liber Pallidus*, and in time my diligence was rewarded. I found the lost *ür*-text of the Grey Book (in the wine cellar of a fortress in Carpatho-Ruthenia—an amusing story, worth telling over brandy and cigars, but not germane to my present communication), and bent my energies toward transcribing and translating those portions which had been purged from the younger manuscripts.

With some effort, I established that the unknown script in which those sections were written was no cipher, but the alphabet of some ancient and now-unspoken tongue. I persevered, hunting down the meaning of the words in spite of their unfamiliarity—seeking out known scripts and alphabets of similar appearance, comparing the shapes and the arrangements of the letters, striving always to bring together sound and sense and ultimate meaning.

By the time I had reached my new goal, that of being able to translate and understand the recovered portions of the Grey Book, the rumblings of political events in my natal land had called me hence from fair Europa. I am a scholar, to be sure, but not one of the type who regards academia as a hermitage, and holds himself aloof from the struggles of the day. If great events were in train, I desired to be a part of them.

It was on that account that in the spring of 1859 I wrote to you with my initial proposal for a revolutionary new source of motive power, drawn from the energy of elemental spirits. My readings in the full text of the *Liber Pallidus* had convinced me that this was the knowledge that the Renaissance savants had purposely lost; the metaphysical studies I had undertaken while searching for the lost portions of the book enabled me to develop the recovered techniques even further.

From the beginning I had known that my goals would be best furthered by the impressment of a spirit of air. The fiery spirits are beings of great puissance, but not to be lightly trusted around gunpowder, or around anything of wooden construction; and their bellicose nature, once roused to a blood-hunger, is not easily controlled. The spirits of earth are heavy and sullen, and indisposed toward cooperation with others not of their kind, while those of water are at best a fickle lot. Air is the only way.

In the autumn of last year, I took the funds you had so kindly invested and used them to put together an expedition above the Arctic Circle. Could I have driven northward as far as the Pole itself, so much would have been the better for my intentions, but even failing that—as in fact happened—the clear air and the unceasing night provided close to an ideal environment for my workings.

When we reached a latitude and longitude which I determined to be suitable, I ordered the other members of the expedition to retreat to our previous encampment, and not to return until at least a week had passed. They did so, leaving me with a winter shelter constructed primarily of snow and canvas. I lost no time in commencing the work.

I shall not speak overmuch of my toils. A large area of smooth ice had first to be inscribed with circles and sigils carved with sharp metal before being picked out in charcoal: hard labor in the cold night, and hazardous for a man working alone, but not so hazardous as the projected work itself, which carried with it risks to both flesh and soul.

In order to accomplish my goal, I would have to complete not one, but two rituals, the first to make ready a temporary housing for an elemental spirit, and the second to draw an elemental into the circle and subject it to my will. Before I could think of doing either, I would have to undergo several days of fasting and meditation. The food supplies that my men had left behind would do little except tempt me—so after I had finished the physical work of making the circle, and had eaten a final meal, I burned them.

My resolve was fixed. Either I would succeed in binding an elemental to my service, or I would perish in the attempt.

I withdrew into my shelter, and gave myself over to the esoteric ritual, not heard beneath the sky in half a thousand years. I had with me a vial of clear glass that I myself had created, small enough to fit into a pocket, with a golden stopper affixed to the neck by a cord. It was but a little container for something as large and formless as an elemental of air, but according to the Grey Book it should suffice until I could perform the further and less harrowing rites needed to transfer the spirit into a more capacious permanent housing.

When I had completed all the mental exercises set forth in the Grey Book—a matter that took some time—I detached myself enough from the work to assess the vial, and was pleased to see that to my inner eye it glowed with the aura of successful consecration and reinforcement. This was good. I was tired, also, as though I had spent a whole day lifting and moving heavy things. I put aside the exhaustion as a matter of no consequence, and sank back into meditation.

This time, I worked to make myself ready for the greater task of calling and compelling the elemental. Time passed; I did not count the days or the hours, but focused my effort and attention on the coming ritual. When I judged that I was ready, I took a sword and a thurible and the glass bottle with me out of the shelter, and went to the circle I had prepared some days before.

The weather had remained clear during the time I had spent in meditation; no snow had fallen to obscure the pattern I had cut into the ice. I placed the stoppered bottle in the center of the circle— taking infinite care not to disturb any of the charcoaled lines—and retreated again to the edge. I had set the incense in the thurible alight before I left the shelter; now I took it up and began walking the circle's outer perimeter, intoning the first staves of the invocation as I did so.

When I had made three complete circuits in this fashion, I stopped, set the thurible down beside me, and used the sword's edge to unleash the hot flow of my own blood. The blood flowed copiously; I stretched out my hand over the circle in the ice and let the drops of liquid fall onto the charcoal-filled grooves beneath. Within seconds, the entire pattern glowed bright red. I let my voice rise into a shout.

"Come down!" I cried out, in the language of the Grey Book, which I will not reproduce here. The old savants were right, I think, to keep it hidden. *"I name you—I seize you—I compel you! Come down and enter the place that I have prepared for you!"*

This was the sticking point. If I failed, I would not have the strength to try again, or even to hold out until the men of my expedition returned. Quite possibly, I would not survive the failure long enough to die waiting for them—the spirits of air may not be so aggressive as those of fire, nor as coldly vengeful as those of earth or sea, but their anger when roused is nonetheless sudden and strong, and nothing of elemental nature bears compulsion lightly.

The glowing red lines that bounded the circle pulsed first bright then dim then bright again. In its center, the glass bottle began to vibrate and glow.

"My will is strong!" I shouted. In the ancient language, the ritual words rose up toward the night sky as an ululating shriek. *"My preparations are complete! Come down, I compel you, come down!"*

The glass bottle shone blue-white like a captured star, and the red lines of the circle roared up into a chest-high wall of flame. Everything paused for a moment—light, flame, voice, heartbeat, everything. Then there was a quiet popping noise, and all the light died. I had barely enough strength left to seize the glass bottle and drag it and myself together inside the shelter. The stars vanished. Snow fell.

The rest of the expedition found me upon their return. They tell me that I was more dead than alive, but even in that state I would not relinquish my hold upon the vial which held what I had so laboriously won. Even now it sits before me, pleasing to my eye.

Thus I have fulfilled the first part of our great project, precisely as promised. What comes next is a matter for further discussion; to which end, if you are willing, we should confer upon my return to New York, which should take place within a few days. Until then I remain, of course,

Your ob't s'v't,
Wm. R. Sharps, Ph.D.

The narrative of Lieutenant John Nevis, USN, continued.

ALTHOUGH I WAS NOT OBLIGATED BY MY ORDERS to do so, I had myself placed on the *Triumph*'s watch bill. I stood my watches on the quarterdeck observing the sea, listening to the crack of canvas, hearing the groans of the cordage, and tasting the salt spray on my lips. I had languished too long on shore, and the uncrowded expanse of the ocean was balm to my soul.

The high North Atlantic in winter is no easy sea, nor was this passage completely peaceful. For twenty-four hours at one point we battled mountainous seas under storm-jib alone, while Uncle Joe stood on the quarterdeck as if he were rooted there, using all his skill to see us through.

Still, a week and a day after our departure from New York, light came without a sun, and we sailed through chilling mist so thick that it might be cotton wool, so thick that the foremast was not visible from the wheel—the sails dropping and the only sound the bell struck by the quartermaster as he turned the glass each half hour.

"We're close now," Uncle Joe said, and instructed the boatswain to commence sounding. Thus we proceeded, making bare steerageway, for most of the day, the fog never lifting, but occasional bits of ice floating by on the sullen swell.

Toward the end of the forenoon watch, a voice from out of the mist cried "Ship ahoy!" and the lookout sang back, "United States Brig *Triumph*!"

With a plash of oars a cutter came alongside and passed us a line, and within an hour, as dark was falling, I found myself standing on a wooden pier attached to a stony shore. Through the mist nothing else could be seen save a warehouse, a heap of coal, and, incredibly, an ornate railway station. A single track ran beside it, and a locomotive attached to a passenger car and ten flatcars stood waiting.

I entered the station in search of both warmth and enlightenment. Once within, I was gratified to find a jolly potbellied stove nearly red from the fire that burned inside it, and a Navy petty officer sitting at a desk. I saw that his hat bore the ribbon "*Nicodemus*," so I strode up to him and inquired where the ship of that name might be found, that I might present my orders.

"A bit of a trip yet, sir," he replied. "First, I must ask if you are carrying any gold or silver, or any items made of iron."

"Why, yes, all three," I said.

"Before you can board the train for the yards," the

man said, "I must ask you to leave them here. For
your silver and gold money I will exchange green-
backs. For watches and rings you will be given a re-
ceipt. As well as your sword, any pistols, and so on."

This was most unusual, but in the course of my
career the Navy had asked many unusual things of
me. The man was sober and serious in aspect, so I
complied.

"I suppose the nails in my boots will pass muster?" I said with a smile.

"No, sir. I must ask you to leave them behind as
well. We've felt boots, sir, and warmer they are than
standard issue." He reached beneath his desk and
pulled out a pair. "Here, sir, let me make your re-
ceipt, and I'll put all your goods in the lockroom
with the rest."

Stripped of money and weapons, and re-shod, I
passed through the other door of the station to the
platform, and onto the passenger car. The words
DEPARTMENT OF THE NAVY, THULE SHIPYARDS were
painted along its side. I could see my brass cannon
being loaded onto the flatcars. At last I was to find
out what manner of vessel I had been assigned to,
and whence the mystery. I noted that the locomotive also was made of brass, as were the rails on
which it stood.

Without my watch I could no longer tell the elapsed
time, but it was not much longer ere the locomotive
gave a lurch and we were underway.

I was the only officer in the railway car. Some
half-dozen other men rode with me, bluejackets

wearing the uniform of *Nicodemus* and the sullen expressions of men returning from liberty. If that railway station was the only place they had to go for entertainment, small wonder that they looked dour. I did not speak to them, nor they to each other, and truth to say I dozed. I suppose the trip lasted some hours.

Nights are long in the far northern latitudes, and it was still dark when a whistle from the locomotive and a slowing of the train announced that we were nearing our destination.

With a final chuff of steam and squeal of brakes we came to a halt. I stood, shouldering my bag, and stepped from the car. The air was thick with mist, and curiously lighted. A pervasive glare surrounded the station, a twin to the one where I had embarked. I soon saw that the flare came from gas lamps set on brass poles, one every twenty feet or so. Somewhere out in the dark, there would be the rounded, cupola-topped bulk of a gas-house, but I could not see it—or, indeed, any structure save the railway station itself—through the all-enswathing fog.

I walked back along the platform to inspect my cargo. The crates were covered by a rime of ice perhaps an inch and a half thick. As I watched, a working party appeared, ghostlike in the fog, with wagons and teams of horses, their breath steaming into the mist. They began working to shift the crates. The utter rapidity of all the evolutions I had witnessed so far, combined with the silence in which they labored, impressed me.

The liberty party had by this time debarked the train as well to shuffle through the station. I turned to follow them. I had no desire to get lost in the cold and fog on an unfamiliar base.

Wherever the sailors were going, they went quickly, without the roistering that is almost universal at fleet landing. What I found on the other side of the station was a long wall, half again as tall as a man, broken by a gate whose lintel bore the words THULE EXPERIMENTAL SHIPYARD, then, in smaller letters below, Authorized Personnel Only.

How likely is it, I asked myself, that unauthorized people will find themselves standing here? Indeed, it seemed to me that I stood at the very edge of the world.

For all the ferocity of the warning above the lintel, no guard stood at the gate for me to present my orders to. Nor was there a sign of the group of sailors I had been following. The mist had swallowed them. The light was brighter here, though, and ahead of me I thought I could make out a tapping sound, though what could be producing it I could not tell.

Since my eyes told me nothing, I decided to follow my ears. The ground was all of clean snow, but trampled flat in a welter of footprints leading in every direction.

The fog was thick, as I mentioned. I could scarcely see the poles holding the lights before bumping into one. But the tapping sound ahead of me grew louder, so I persevered. My cheeks were stinging with the cold, and my lungs hurt with the effort of breathing.

Before long I perceived that I was no longer walking on trampled snow but on ice, perfectly smooth. Shortly afterward, I came to the source of the sound: a party of sailors, swinging picks, chipping away at the edge of the ice. Beyond them was black water, and beyond that the smooth sides of a ship. The line of sailors went out of my sight to the right and left. Among them were some with long-handled rakes. When a piece of ice was chipped free, it was swept up and away.

I turned to my right and walked behind the sailors as they engaged in their peculiar task. It seemed as though they were endlessly laboring to keep the ice away from the sides of the vessel. I walked sixty paces before the line of men made a ninety-degrees turn to the left, and I followed it to pass under the ship's bows, then thirty paces after another corner. A third corner took me under her stern. I was not surprised to see the name *Nicodemus* painted in dull gold on the sternboard.

Another turn and thirty more paces brought me to where I supposed I had started, still without a clue as to how I was meant to get aboard the ship. No brow, ladder, or companionway had appeared during my circuit, nor had I seen a boat in the water.

At that moment I saw a light moving on the deck above me, so I sang out, "Hello the ship!"

"Aye aye!" came the answer.

"Lieutenant John Nevis, United States Navy, reporting as ordered for duty aboard USS *Nicodemus*," I shouted back.

"Oh, bugger," replied the voice. "Go to the house and report to the captain in the morning."

"Bugger yourself," I called back, cold, tired, and annoyed. "I haven't a clue where this house might be."

"Hopkins, take the lieutenant in tow and stow him away, would you?" the voice called. A moment later, a young sailor stepped up beside me, saluted, and reached for my seabag.

"You'll learn your way around here quick enough, sir," he said. "But you might as well know that they don't do things here the way they do anywhere else in the fleet."

That I could well believe, though I had no desire to show overfamiliarity with the ordinary seaman by telling him so. I believe Hopkins understood my silence, for without another word he shouldered my bag and started off. I followed, from the ice to a slope, all snow covered, and thence to the porch of a pleasant house of clapboard, its shutters closed tight against the night.

"Here you are, sir," Hopkins said, saluted, then faded away into the fog. For my part I returned the salute, turned the knob, and pushed into the vestibule. The three officers inside the house quickly introduced themselves: Lieutenant Dodge, Lieutenant Vincent, and Ensign Seaton, all line officers. Dodge was the senior man, and first officer for *Nicodemus*;

Vincent was junior, in charge of decks and masts; I myself, with the guns, came third in seniority. Ensign Seaton, for his part, was attached to the yard itself, rather than making one of the ship's complement.

"Come," said Lieutenant Dodge after I had introduced myself. "You must be half frozen and completely tired after your journey. Let me show you to your cabin here ashore."

"Gladly," I replied. "But first, tell me, what manner of place is this?"

"The God-damnedest shipyard that I've ever seen," Dodge replied. "If the Navy needed to build a ship in a dark, cold, and cheerless place, the Portsmouth yards would have served the purpose quite adequately. Lovely duty here; there's a girl behind every tree."

"I did not see any trees . . ." I began, then quieted.

Dodge shouldered my seabag, and led the way up the stairs to a corridor on the upper floor. Seaton followed with a kerosene lamp. He opened the first door on the right, and we all followed in.

The furnishings were spare, but adequate, with two narrow beds, a washstand, two desks, two chairs, and two wardrobes. A register in the floor let heat from the fire below flow up, though not much of it; the exterior wall's inner face glittered with ice.

"This bunk is mine," Dodge said, pointing to the one closest to the window, "and that clothes press. Stow your gear where you will."

He lighted a candle from the lamp, then he and Seaton departed, pulling the door closed behind them.

I could see my breath in the air of the room. Nevertheless, the bed looked entirely inviting. I stood my seabag in the wardrobe, hung my clothing over the back of a chair, blew out the candle, and by feel alone crawled between the cold sheets. I said my prayers while curled in a ball, only my nose sticking out, and soon fell asleep.

What seemed an instant later, a tremendous hammering fell on the door. I started upright. The window was as black as it had been when I arrived.

Before I could say a word, an enlisted man in a pea coat and gloves entered, and placed a lighted lamp on the near desk.

"Good morning, sir," he said, but did not stay for reply, instead tramping out and shutting the door behind him.

I rose and dressed, wearing the same clothes I had traveled in, and with lamp in hand descended to the drawing room where I had encountered the other three officers the night before.

Some hours had apparently passed. The card party had been cleared away, and the three officers I had previously met were dressed with coats and gloves of their own. My coat was over my arm, and I donned it now, after first placing the lamp on the table.

Two other officers had joined the others I already knew, bringing our company to six.

"Ah, there you are," Dodge said. He had been

consulting a small notebook, which he replaced in his inner pocket as I arrived. "Off to break our fast. Join us?"

"With pleasure," I said, for my last meal had been a hasty one while still coming to land the day before.

"Come on, then. You can tell us the latest news of the war while we eat—there's no newspaper or telegraph, as you can imagine, and no letters to come or go."

"What, none?"

"Not a line," said Dodge. "The Thule Shipyard doesn't exist; and neither do we, so long as we're here."

No wonder the sailors on the train had appeared so glum and silent, I thought, but I said nothing. The six of us went out of the door, down the steps, and made our way in a gaggle across the creaking snow to a long and low structure, where smoke rose from chimneys at each end and a line of windows glowed yellow.

We entered, Dodge in the lead, and walked between tables flanked by benches, all filled with sailors eating their morning portions. We proceeded to a spot halfway down where a thin partition set off a single table with chairs.

One officer was already there, a sheaf of papers under his hand—ship's plans, from the look of them. He glanced up when we all arrived, rolling the plans and placing them in a case leaning against the partition.

"Welcome to the mess," Dodge said. "Time for introductions all around."

These were quickly performed. The gentlemen I had not met the evening before were two more ensigns, by the names of Williams and Bash, and the officer already at the table was a lieutenant named Cromwell. The last named was a lean and bespectacled individual, a graduate of the Academy and latterly of France's l'École Polytechnique; I was given to know that he was the engineering officer aboard *Nicodemus*.

"I viewed the ship briefly on my arrival," I said to Cromwell, "and did not see sidewheels or a sternwheel on her. Will you be using an Ericsson screw, or are the wheels not yet mounted?"

"Propulsion is no concern of yours," was all he replied.

*From the private diary
of Miss Columbia Abrams.*

MARCH 6TH, 1863

HAVING BROKEN OUR JOURNEY BRIEFLY IN PHILA-delphia, we are once again on our way to New York.

So far, little of note has taken place—I do not intend for this journal to be nothing more than a foolish diary of fashions and flirtations, so there is no point to writing here about the paisley shawl I purchased at Mr. Wanamaker's new store, or about the many young men in uniform who crowd the railway cars between Washington and New York.

Instead, I shall take the occasion to explain, for the benefit of whatever distant posterity may someday read these pages, how my involvement with this enterprise came about.

In the summer of 1862, Father and I were living in Washington, where he had traveled from Boston in the spring of '61 to assist the Secretary of War in the coming crisis, and where I had joined him upon my graduation from the Hadley Female Academy. I was unhappy and restless. I missed the fellowship of my bosom friends at the Academy, now scattered across the broken Union; I disliked the capital city's muggy and oppressive climate; and I had nothing to do save entertain suitors who never came, and act as my father's hostess for parties he never gave.

I did my best to hide my discontent. It was not Father's fault that the war and politics took up all of his time, with nothing left over for sociability, or that all the young men in Washington were either working for the government themselves and were therefore as busy as he was, or were in the military and even busier. A few of the younger men made some attempt to cultivate our acquaintance, but Father did not encourage them, and in the face of his indifference their enthusiasm soon waned.

Nevertheless, Father saw my unhappiness, and when he told me that he had invited the eminent Mr. Vanderbilt and his good friend Mr. Sharps to our rented house in Georgetown for a friendly dinner, I thought at first that he meant it as a treat. Even great men, after all, may have wives and daughters of congenial disposition. I threw myself on the mercy of our cook, and together she and I devised a menu which—we hoped!—would not disgrace the household in front of its distinguished visitors.

Mr. Vanderbilt and Mr. Sharps arrived promptly at the stated dinner hour. Upon first learning that there were to be no other guests, I had asked Father if he would prefer that I not join them, but he told me most emphatically that I should attend—that my presence had been, in fact, specifically requested.

The news filled me with a trepidation that my first sight of Messrs. Vanderbilt and Sharps did nothing to dispel. The Commodore, as he was known from his many shipping and transportation interests, had grey hair and fierce white whiskers; Mr. Sharps was clean-shaven, and to my mind had an air about him of Shakespeare's Cassius—he of the "lean and hungry look." He had lank blond hair tinged with silver, and eyes of a peculiar shade of pale blue, the color of a summer sky hazed over by the first high clouds of a distant storm.

The meal passed in unexceptional conversation. After Susie, the kitchen maid, had carried away the remains of dessert—a *vol-au-vent* of whipped cream and strawberries that Cook had worked on all afternoon—I rose to take my leave.

Father halted me with a gesture. "Please join us in the study, Columbia," he said.

"See here, Abrams," Mr. Vanderbilt broke in. "I told you we needed to get a look at the girl—that was all."

"She needs to know everything. Otherwise, this goes no further."

I thought for a moment that Mr. Vanderbilt would be angry—everything I had ever heard or read about him said that he was *not* a man who enjoyed being crossed or thwarted—but Father only sat and looked at him calmly, just as if the Commodore were not someone who could break any man in the country if it entered his mind to.

"Very well," Mr. Vanderbilt said after a moment.

I let myself start breathing properly again, and the four of us left the dining room together.

In Father's study, the lamp was turned low and the curtains were drawn tight. Father said to Mr. Vanderbilt, in an apologetic tone, "I thought it best not to call outside attention to our conversation here."

"Prudent, Mr. Abrams," said Mr. Sharps. It was the first time he had spoken since the end of dinner; he had watched the exchange between Father and the Commodore with an expression at once interested and detached. "Are the servants likewise reliable?"

"Not a Rebel sympathizer among them," Father said—which was the truth, as it happens, though I was the only one who had spoken with them enough to be sure.

Mr. Vanderbilt frowned. "See to it, William."

Mr. Sharps went to the study door and traced something with his finger on the wood, then crossed the room and did the same to the drawn curtains. I felt my skin prickle the way it used to in the dormitory at Hadley, whenever Annabel Parker set a mark of silence on the door so that we could gossip deep into the night with no one hearing.

Something of what I felt must have shown in my

countenance, for I observed that Mr. Vanderbilt was watching me intently.

"She perceives it, William," he said. He turned to my father. "My congratulations to you, Mr. Abrams. If your daughter proves as diligent as she is virtuous, she will do well."

Mr. Sharps gave me a cold look. "Her school should have trained her, if she was suited for the curriculum."

"Hadley Female Academy doesn't teach the metaphysical arts to its undergraduates," I said.

"Still, you recognized the marks."

I tried not to show my gratification at being thus addressed directly. If there is anything more tiresome than being talked *about* in front of one's face, just as if one were a farm animal or a piece of furniture, then I do not wish to experience it.

"One of my classmates knew how to set them," I said. "I don't know where she learned."

"Did she teach them to you?"

"No, sir," I said. Annabel and I had known the difference between rules that were safe to break (provided that we were willing, if caught, to bear the punishment) and rules that were not—but I said nothing of that, as the Commodore and Mr. Sharps did not strike me as men who would care overmuch about the ways and thoughts of schoolgirls.

"Good. Since I have barely six months to teach you everything that is necessary, the less you know to begin with, the less you will need to unlearn."

This conversation, I thought, was growing stranger and stranger, as if there were things in it that everyone knew about except me. I drew myself together and put on my best dignity. "I'm afraid I don't understand, sir."

The Commodore made a disdainful noise, as though my lack of understanding were a deliberate affront, and Father said, "It's a long story, Columbia, but I promise you that I will explain everything before we are finished here tonight. For now, though, I believe that it's enough to say your country needs you. Will you accept the challenge?"

My breath caught a little at the question. I tried not to let too much emotion show in my face as I made my reply, lest the strength of my sentiments be mistaken for mere girlish effusion.

"I may be a woman," I said, "but I love my country as much, I think, as any man."

"Are you willing to face danger and endure privation on her behalf?" Mr. Vanderbilt asked.

His voice suggested that he doubted my fortitude and resolution were equal to the task—and this, I fear, prompted me to further recklessness. Even as a schoolgirl I could never refuse a dare.

"You have but to try me, sir," I said, "and you will soon see that I am willing."

Mr. Vanderbilt laughed and said, "You have the right spirit, girl—that's for sure. But what Sharps, here, needs is a girl who's *un*-tried and *un*-willing."

My father bristled up at him. "You are speaking to my daughter, sir!"

"Yes, yes," said Mr. Sharps calmly. "And her maiden blushes testify in her behalf. If her learning and her abilities prove as reliable as her virtue, then I believe she will serve our enterprise well."

From a sealed letter from Jean-Claude Lesquignard, captain of the French unarmored sailing cruiser Pallas, *to Napoléon Samuel Prosper de Chasseloup-Laubat, Ministre de la Marine.*

12 MARCH—1863

MY LORD,—I HAVE THE HONOR TO INFORM YOU OF a most unusual and disturbing phenomenon.

On the 11th day of the current month, we had lain for three days becalmed at 60°20' North/32°08' West in patchy fog. We had seen no other vessel during this time, nor for some days preceding, and had heard no bell or gong sounding through the fog bank save our own. At two bells of the morning watch on the day in question, I was breakfasting alone in my cabin when a runner brought word that the officer of the deck urgently requested my presence. Greatly curious as to what might be the cause of such a summons, I abandoned my morning coffee and made haste to join Lieutenant Morin on *Pallas's* starboard quarterdeck, where the following conversation then took place:

Myself: Well, Lieutenant. What have we here?

Lieutenant Morin: Behold yonder—something approaches in the mist.

Myself: I see nothing, Lieutenant.

Lieutenant Morin: It withdraws itself, and then returns. See! Now it comes again.

I looked in the direction the lieutenant was pointing. For a moment I saw nothing save scraps of fog above the water. Then I glimpsed a fleeting motion in the clouds, like a blur in the eye, a darker object against the grey. At times it took on a more definite shape, only to once again blur into a mist.

Myself: I see. It would appear to be a ship.

Lieutenant Morin: But what manner of craft, to move at such a rate of speed when there is no wind, and without smoke or the sound of engines?

Myself: By God, Lieutenant, I cannot tell. Let us watch her closely and see what reveals.

We continued thus in observation for a quarter of an hour. The mysterious vessel behaved as Lieutenant Morin had said, approaching at times close enough that the line of her black hull could almost be discerned through the fog, and at other times seeming to vanish with the quickness of illusion.

If this is a ship—I spoke thus to Lieutenant Morin—then it is such as the world has never before seen, and if we had a favorable wind I would strive to bring *Pallas* near enough to see her clearly.

It was as if the other had heard my wish, and

moved on a whim to grant it. The vessel, that had been until now keeping itself to a distance in the fog, changed course and began to draw steadily closer, on a straight line across our bows, making an apparent speed of six to eight knots. Observing this development, Lieutenant Morin and I made our way to the forecastle, and once again exchanged words:

Lieutenant Morin: What happens now?

Myself: It would appear that her captain desires, after all, to be seen.

Lieutenant Morin: Why now, and not before?

Myself: Perhaps he has determined that we neither present danger nor give opportunity. Or perhaps for some other reason that we may know shortly.

The ship continued toward us out of the mist, and soon drew near enough for her rigging and armaments to be discerned without the aid of a glass. She appeared to be a second-class sloop of war, a square-rigged three-master, of twenty guns. Her bow was sharp, her counter straight, narrow in the beam, her masts severely raked, and her freeboard low. She bore a single cabin aft, white in color. While her poop was flush with the main deck, she had a raised forecastle surmounted by a structure not unlike an Aegyptian pyramid.

What her method of propulsion might be, I found myself unable to determine. Despite the rapidity of her progress in the flat calm, she carried no sail and had no funnel, no wheel to churn the water, nor did I see or smell smoke. She bore no figurehead nor ornamentation on her bow, but her bare masts and yards appeared to be sheathed in light grey metal—tin, perhaps, though the luster was more nearly that of silver. No sails were rigged, nor even furled. The flag the sloop flew at her main top was that of the American Confederacy.

I directed Lieutenant Morin to hail her, and he did so, but there was no response, nor did I observe any sailors on her decks. The black sloop passed across our bows in silence, no more than a pistol shot away, maintaining her course and speed all the while. The waves cast up by the vessel's passage rocked us as she headed off once more into the fog. The name picked out in silver on her sternboard was *Alecto.*

Lieutenant Morin then indicated the water ahead of us and said: Look there, captain.

I did so, and saw a dozen or more sharks following in *Alecto*'s wake, their fins cutting the water and their dark bodies at times leaping entirely free of the waves. Lieutenant Morin said: What does this mean, sir?

By God, I said to him—and I say to you also, my lord, as I make this report on what I have observed—by God, sir, I do not know.

*The narrative of Lieutenant
John Nevis, USN, continued.*

I WAS TAKEN ABACK BY THE CURTNESS OF THE
engineering officer's reply, but said nothing. Junior
officers—as I at the time still was—are enjoined to
be the best listeners in the room. As the newest
member of *Nicodemus*'s wardroom it behooved me
to observe without speaking, and to refrain from
making a bad first impression that could make my
entire tour of duty unpleasant.

Further interaction was cut short by the arrival of
food. It was plain but hot, and that was all I required
at the time. I had drunk worse coffee during my career. Williams and Bash were supply corps—Williams attached to the shipyard, and Bash to the ship
itself—and so worth knowing. I complimented them
on the quality of the breakfast, and they seemed
cheered.

"Whatever else is lacking," Williams said, "the
Navy has seen fit to provision us well. Trainloads of

provender, and a warehouse bigger than the ship to hold it."

"A soft berth, then," I said. "If not for the cold and dark."

"A bit too soft, if you ask me," said Vincent. "The war could be over before any of us see action."

"I think not," I replied. "The government would scarcely have troubled itself with sending a dozen Rodmans to the far ends of the earth if there wasn't a need for them."

"Your news is fresher than any of ours," Dodge said. "How do matters stand with the Union?"

I gave them the best summary that I could. *Triumph*'s previous supply run had brought them news by word of mouth concerning our army's dear-bought victory at Antietam Creek—the source, so far as I could determine, of Lieutenant Vincent's opinions concerning the imminent cessation of hostilities—but they had heard nothing of its subsequent humiliation before Fredericksburg. Of the exploits of Admirals Dixon and Farragut upon the Mississippi they had received some rumor (the Navy being ever more talkative about its own), but I was able to provide some further detail. As for President Lincoln's proclamation of freedom for all those held in slavery in the Rebel states, they had received no word at all until I brought it to them.

One further thing had been gnawing at my mind as we talked. "I should like to call on the captain," I said, "as soon as might be. What is his name, and where might I find him?"

"I'll bring you to Captain Sharps before long, in his quarters," Dodge said. "You'll learn more then."

I was beginning to grow apprehensive, but considered that the feeling might be caused by the oppressive dark, and by the lack of clocks. The Navy is regulated by clocks and time; without them navigation is impossible. Yet here, where I supposed that the sun might rise eventually, clocks did not regulate the day, and nothing seemed to measure the passage of the hours. Perhaps, I thought, they used sandglasses.

Upon finishing breakfast, the officers rose as a group, and I with them. "Come with me," Dodge said, and when the rest turned at the door toward the officers' quarters, we went the other way, to the left, toward yet another house, with light showing in all its windows. The enshrouding mist had blown off while I slept, although there was now scarcely a breeze.

We entered the house without knocking, advancing through a short hall to a room on the right-hand side. A coal grate burned there, warming the room. A table stood nearby, spread with plans and blueprints; shelves of ledgers covered the walls; and a builder's half-model lay against the wall below the window. The only decoration on the wall was a printed calendar, on which the days of the month were printed in black and the days from the beginning of the year were printed in red. Annotations in a careful hand filled each of the numbered squares.

I looked questioningly at Dodge. He nodded

toward the far inner door, then turned and left.

Nothing for it, I thought, strode to the door and rapped sharply on the frame.

"What?" came a voice from the far side, one surprisingly high and mild. I had been, I suppose, expecting the hoarse roar of a seadog.

"Lieutenant John Nevis, reporting for duty, as ordered," I said. I had my hat tucked under my left arm, and was withdrawing the many-times folded copy of my orders from my inner pocket with my right hand as I spoke.

"Enter," came the tenor voice.

I twisted the knob and pushed the door open, then took a pace in.

The captain sat at a desk, the remnants of his breakfast on a tray on the floor beside him. He laid the feather of a seabird, a long, grey feather, on the pages of the book before him, and closed it. Before the book closed, I could see that it was handwritten rather than printed, and that a diagram of a pentalpha graced the verso page that he had been studying.

"What is it?" the captain asked, looking at me with clear blue eyes. His hair was a pale blond, somewhat thinning, brushed carefully back from a high forehead. Despite his rank, which should have implied a considerable length of service, he was not a man I knew either personally or by reputation, making him an anomaly in the small world of the naval officer corps, and leading me to suspect that he had been commissioned directly from his calling in civilian life. A strange captain for a strange ship, I thought, but wartime has its exigencies.

"I am assigned to *Nicodemus* as gunnery officer," I said, and offered him my sheet of orders.

Captain Sharps did not take them, only giving them a quick glance and gesturing that I should put them away. I refolded the papers and tucked them inside the crown of my hat for safekeeping. The captain regarded me with a steady, measuring gaze.

"You brought the guns?" he asked.

"Yes, sir. Twelve nine-inch Rodmans."

"Very well. See to their mounting." He turned back to his desk.

"One thing, Captain," I said, although he had clearly intended to dismiss me.

"Yes?" he looked up, and although I had just met the man I could sense his annoyance.

"I do not possess gunnery tables for brass cannon and brass shot. Before mounting all the guns, I should like to experiment with one away from the ship, to determine the lay and loading."

"See to it," the Captain said.

With that, I was definitely dismissed. I turned and departed.

The sky outside was still black, and pierced by the diamond-bright stars of a high northern altitude. With the mist gone, I could see that the entire area around the ship was brightly lit, with more lights around the railway, the warehouses, and the other parts of the yard. Down around *Nicodemus* the working party labored endlessly with their picks, keeping open the water.

I turned back toward the officers' quarters and commenced walking. The cold was intense, and only motion seemed to ameliorate it.

As I walked, I met Lieutenant Vincent, standing on one of the more beaten tracks amid the trampled snow.

"Good morning," he called as I approached and after we had traded salutes.

"Good morning," I replied. "Do you suppose I could trouble you to show me about? I am particularly interested in seeing the armory and bunker and, if possible, touring the ship."

"I believe that I can break free long enough to do so," he said.

We fell in step, walking away from the captain's house and past officers' quarters. All at once he stopped.

"What is it?" I asked.

By way of reply he nodded to the right.

Over the snow I saw a column approach, of silent men, dressed in thick felts, carrying tools slung over their backs or in pouches along their waists. They wore slouch hats, and their long grey beards swung to and fro with every pace. They did not look to right nor left, nor did their eyes look anywhere other than straight ahead. If not for their moving legs and swinging beards they might have been statues.

Indeed, my first thought was of automata, but they were clearly men of flesh. They continued at a steady pace toward *Nicodemus*. I had the impression that if we had attempted to cross in front of them, they would have trampled us.

"What are they?" I asked Vincent after the group had passed. The word "What" seemed more apt than "who."

"Civilian yard workers," Vincent replied. "Mr. Dodge has a tale to tell of 'em, if you ask."

I let the silence lengthen, but he did not elaborate; we walked onward.

Soon enough we came to a windowless building. The short end held a large door, like a barn door, and a smaller door beside it. Opening the smaller door led to a short hallway with another door at the far end. Once through that, the place opened out, revealing crates and boxes arrayed between the posts that held up the roof. A desk, wooden, with a kerosene lamp providing light, stood before us, and a petty officer dressed in a thick monkey jacket and watch cap sat at the desk.

He rose to his feet as we entered.

"As you were," Vincent said. "Where are the new guns that arrived last night?"

"This way, sir," the petty officer said.

He picked up the lamp and led us down a corridor between the crates. At the far end of the structure he stopped, beside another barn door. The interior wall sparkled with ice, and snow lay on the floor here. My dozen crates lay on the floor beside one another. I was struck by how they looked like coffins, lined up on a railway siding. It was only a momentary impression.

"Open one," I said. "I wish to see how it survived the trip."

The petty officer placed his lamp on an adjacent ledge while he pried the lid of one of the cannon crates. The lid of the crate came up with a squeal of nails; I took up the lamp to look more closely at the cannon. It lay, trunnions boxed in, the chase supported by more blocks, muzzle and breech touching the inner surfaces of the packing crate. I reached out my hand toward it.

Lieutenant Vincent stopped me. "Probably best not to touch it, without thicker gloves," he said. "Laying bare flesh on anything metal at all can be dangerous here. You'll stick right to it."

"Indeed," I replied. "Be that as it may, I must get at least one of these thunderers rigged here ashore, to get an idea of the fall of shot from them, and to give my gun crews a bit of training."

"Of course," Vincent said.

"May I see the ship now?"

"You may, though you may be disappointed," he said.

I handed the lamp back to the petty officer. He led our way back to the front of the building.

Nicodemus herself looked much the same as she had the night before, even to the color of the sky, an inky black. The lights still burned, the sailors still chipped the ice to clear the water. From the ship herself I could hear the sounds of hammers as the yard workers performed their tasks. A boat boom was swung out to starboard, and from it a Jacob's ladder depended, stopping some feet above the surface of the ice.

"Here we are," Vincent said. "On the ice pack we can't really build a pier or a proper brow."

He led the way, climbing the edge as nimbly as any foremast hand, until he stood on the boat boom looking down. "You need to be careful on the way across," he said, as I climbed after him. "The water is devilish cold. Any man who falls in must be rescued in a minute, or he is lost, and he is incapable of aid in his own behalf."

"Lost one, have you?" said I, having gained the top of the boom.

"More than one," Vincent said. He left the words hanging in the frozen air as he turned and walked along the boom toward the waist. I saw that nothing from the ship touched the ice, not even the Jacob's ladder.

*From the private diary
of Miss Columbia Abrams.*

MARCH 10TH, 1863

FATHER AND I HAVE REACHED NEW YORK. WE ARE lodged at Mr. Vanderbilt's expense in the Fifth Avenue Hotel on Madison Square, awaiting the return to port of USS *Triumph*, the ship which is to carry me from here to a point above the Arctic Circle, there to join with Mr. Sharps and his metaphysical vessel.

The hotel is a grand place, a marble building with enough rooms, I am told, for eight hundred guests. The journey to our accommodations on the fourth floor was an adventure in itself. We did not need to climb the stairs; the hotel's famous perpendicular railway, with many shakings and judderings, conveyed us upward. Nor did we need to exert ourselves afterward to search for a nearby restaurant: Shortly after our arrival, a hotel porter brought in a tray laden with covered dishes.

I looked at the chicken in aspic adorned with what could only be truffles and said to my father, "Mr. Vanderbilt is sparing no expense on our behalf."

"Say rather, on your behalf," my father replied. "My presence here is merely to insure your safe arrival aboard the *Triumph*. What you see about you is the least expense he could imagine for his purpose. If he could have accomplished the same thing at lower cost by sending you through the government mail like a parcel, I do believe he would have done so."

"I admit, when I met him he did not seem like a man in the habit of doing favors for others out of the pure goodness of his heart." I paused long enough to savor the first bite of the chicken my father sliced for me—the truffles, I found, were not what I had expected, but I think I might learn to appreciate the flavor—then said, "To tell the truth, I'm not sure why Mr. Vanderbilt is doing any of this. It cannot possibly turn a profit."

My father looked thoughtful. "No, but it may well gain him something he wants even more than money."

"And what is that?"

"Revenge."

"Revenge? You make him sound a veritable Titus Andronicus."

"He is certainly enough larger than life to be one," my father said. "The story, as I understand it, is this: A dozen years or so ago, Mr. Vanderbilt decided that the best way to make a profit from the western gold-fields was to enter the business of getting people to

California; he first grew wealthy as a ferryman in his youth, so I suppose he saw transport as a surer thing than washing nuggets out of mountain streams. The Commodore received an exclusive charter from the government of Nicaragua to convey passengers across their country from the Atlantic Ocean to the Pacific. His Accessory Transit Company, as he named it, provided the fastest route from New York to San Francisco—by steamship to the east coast of Nicaragua, across Nicaragua by riverboat and stagecoach, then by ship again from the west coast of Nicaragua. The route was safer than rounding Cape Horn or trekking across the Rocky Mountains, with Vanderbilt controlling the middle leg and setting the fares. With gold fever burning strong in those days and every westward traveler hoping to be the first to stake a claim, the company made money hand over fist."

"This happy condition cannot have persisted," I said. "Else there would be no further story."

"Just so. Two years later, Mr. Vanderbilt determined to make an extended tour of Europe. He left the running of Accessory Transit in the hands of a pair of trusted subordinates: Charles Morgan and C. K. Garrison. Naturally, they betrayed him."

"Naturally," I said. "I don't think I shall marry a man of business, father. The sort of man who would betray a business partner would also betray a wife."

"There's no need to be thinking of such things for a while yet," he said. "You are still young. As for Mr.

Morgan and Mr. Garrison, they entered into a pact with a man named William Walker—"

"The president of Nicaragua?"

My father's features assumed a look of disgust. "As he styles himself. At the time, he was but a penniless adventurer with grand ambitions—and, though we did not then know it, the beginnings of dark knowledge. Morgan and Garrison gave Walker twenty thousand dollars with which to raise a military force and overthrow the Nicaraguan government, and give them control of the overland route from east to west. Walker agreed, for his own purposes. With the aid of certain others who believed that he would bring a conquered Nicaragua into the Union as a slave state, he succeeded in his goal—and promptly revoked the Accessory Transit Company's charter and gave the concession to Morgan and Garrison instead."

"What did Mr. Vanderbilt do?"

" 'The law is slow, gentlemen,' he told his partners. 'I will not sue you; I will ruin you,'—and so he did. He formed a new transit company to take passengers overland through Panama instead of through Nicaragua, then sold the fares at so low a price that he took all the business away from Morgan and Garrison and drove them into bankruptcy. After that, he turned his attention to William Walker; but Walker proved a harder nut to crack. Mr. Vanderbilt gave arms and money to Walker's enemies in Costa Rica, and in British Honduras and Guatemala and San Salvador, to depose the man from his so-called presidency, but their efforts met with disaster upon disaster—epidemics, earthquakes, volcanic mountains spewing flame and noxious vapors—until it became clear that at some point in his wandering life William Walker had found a source of occult learning, and had drunk his fill of its poisoned spring."

"No wonder his country is allied with the Rebels," I said. "Wickedness calls to wickedness."

"He's been a thorn in the side of the Union since before the war began," my father agreed. "But while he may think that Mr. Vanderbilt has contented himself with punishing Morgan and Garrison, the truth is that the Commodore has not forgotten—and has most certainly not forgiven—Walker's role in that offense. Mr. Sharps believes that his ship can somehow do an injury to William Walker, or thwart Walker's plans, and Mr. Vanderbilt will consider any money paid on the project well-spent if Sharps can only carry through on his expectations."

I thought about this. "So Mr. Vanderbilt is acting out of spite and seeks revenge, and Mr. Sharps is acting out of—what? Zeal for knowledge? Pride? Lust for power? Does either of them care a whit for the Union, or for Abolition?"

"I'm afraid," said my father gravely, "that the responsibility for caring about both of those things falls to you."

"I understand," I said, but in truth I was for some time that evening prey to feelings of unease. As I

thought at the time—but did not say to my father—
"How can one fight wickedness with iniquity?" For
sin is sin, and hath one master. A house divided
against itself cannot stand.

The narrative of Lieutenant John Nevis, USN, continued.

ONCE ABOARD *NICODEMUS*, AND HAVING SA-
luted the officer of the deck and the national flag,
Vincent led me forward. The ship was well founded,
though broader in the beam even than the *Tisdale*,
the air permeated by the smell of pine, fir, oak, and
tar that one finds especially on newly constructed
vessels. The air was sharp and the breath steamed in
our noses and mouths as we breathed and talked.

"All the guns to be mounted topside?" I asked,
indicating the attachment points for the gun tackle,
dark bronze and six to a side.

"All of them," Vincent said. "Would you like to
see the spar deck?"

"That I would, as well as the magazine and the
berthing spaces," said I.

"Of course."

So far we had been making our way by the light
that came from those bright lamps on posts rigged

ashore. By now our circuit had taken us back to the area of the quarterdeck. A wheel stood there, just aft of a set of skyports, but no binnacle was mounted. Instead, just forward of the quarterdeck, I espied a circular area marked out by a ring of brass set into the planking.

"What might that be?" I asked, nodding toward the circle.

"No one knows," said Lieutenant Vincent, "save maybe the captain, and he hasn't said aught, except to say that all hands are forbidden to cross it or to step inside it, under pain of the severest punishment allowed by regulations."

"We shall learn its purpose in time, I suppose. But is there no compass aboard *Nicodemus*?"

"No, nor will there be one," Vincent said. "This will make navigation an interesting proposition, as we'll have fewer tools than Columbus had. Nathaniel Bowditch himself would find it a pretty problem."

"Chronometers?"

"Sandglasses only, turned every hour." He picked up a tin kerosene lamp with gloved hands and lighted it with a match drawn from an inner pocket. He tossed the spent match over the side into the black water, then turned again to the ship's centerline.

We found the after hatch, and descended the ladder to port, beside the flag bag. The deck below was lighted by the kerosene lamp that Vincent carried.

A bulkhead stood forward, and we proceeded in that direction.

On the other side of the thin bulkhead, which was white and smelled of new paint, stood the long open spar deck. There racks, now empty, stood ready for their burden of oars, of spars, of canvas and cordage. Brass hooks for the sailors to attach their hammocks from the overhead were already in place.

Our breath still steamed. Here came one of the bearded yard workers, his hand clutching a leather case of tools; hammers and a saw protruded, and a carpenter's square. He passed us silently, no breath-smoke issuing from his lips or nose.

"Do they talk at all?" I asked, after the man had passed.

"Generally, no," he replied. "On those rare occasions when they do speak, their talk is some foreign gabble."

"Ah," I said. "I'd say that not much remains for them to do, at least here."

"We were awaiting only your arrival with the guns," Vincent said.

Another hatch forward took us down to the ship's powder magazine. Though smaller than I would have liked, it seemed well-founded enough, with spark-proof lamps attached to the bulkheads; as elsewhere aboard the ship, a glistening layer of ice crystals sparkled on every surface.

"Is there another magazine?" I asked.

Vincent shook his head. "I believe this is it."

"I'd be happier if the magazine were mounted closer to the waist," I said.

"As would I, but all that area is taken up with machinery rooms, or at least so I'm told."

"You haven't seen them?"

"No. Damned odd, but what about this billet isn't?"

We ascended the ladder, and walked back through the spar deck and thence up to the main deck. A load of timbers had been brought on board, and the yard workers were busy constructing gun carriages. They labored without speaking, the only sounds those of their brass tools. And they worked without light.

The officers' quarters aft were decent. A ladder there descended to the third deck, but a petty officer stood at the head of the ladder and said, "I'm sorry, sir, you can't come this way. Authorized personnel only."

"What do you mean?"

"I'm sorry, sir. Captain's orders," was the man's reply.

"None other than the engineers can go below there," Vincent said, hurrying up. He took me by the elbow and led me away. We went back on deck.

"Can you introduce me to the gunner?" I asked.

"Yes. I believe that I can," Vincent said.

"I will want to construct my test rig ashore at the soonest opportunity."

"Would you look at that," Vincent said. "Light in the sky. I'd forgotten that it was possible."

He was pointing past the *Nicodemus*'s bow, out over the ice field. A grey glow outlined a horizon, the sky a bit less dark than the sea.

"The east?" I asked.

"No, more the south. It's as much daylight as we'll get for a month yet—but still a gladsome sight. Come on, I'll help find you Gunner Bellevue. He's your man."

"Right, then."

We made our way along the boat boom to the Jacob's ladder, and so to the ice. I allowed myself to drop the last few feet, for I had a feeling that it would be unchancy to touch a part of the ship and the land at the same time.

"How was the ship constructed without proper ways?" I asked as we walked back toward the cluster of buildings.

"The keel was laid on the ice," Vincent replied, "and the rest built up. One day the hull grew too heavy for the ice to bear, and it smashed through. How the ice creaked and growled! The water boiled up around it for a bit, then the men were set to removing the ice. They've been doing so ever since."

The remainder of the day was spent in settling myself in and learning the names of my gun captains. One cannon I needed to set up ashore, to test-fire. Accordingly, I spent the afternoon—for sunrise, such as it was, had occurred near to noon and the midday meal—in finding a promising place: flat, near the edge of the ice sheet but not on it, and pointing out over the frozen bay, away from the ship, the buildings, and the usual pathways of men.

*The narrative of Lieutenant
John Nevis, USN, continued.*

YARD-TIME IS, INVARIABLY, DULL. THE MEN MAY
be kept busy with tasks such as rubbing down spun
yarn or, as here, removing ice. But for officers, walking about watching civilians work, men who cannot
be commanded, and without the day's work of navigation to perform, days can be tedious.

The patch of open water in which the ship lay
grew larger. Now the vessel moved forward and
back in a channel, keeping the black water clear of
ice. She moved without sound and without any apparent means of propulsion, forward and back, the
channel growing ever longer and longer.

I busied myself with building my test bed. I obtained a gun carriage from *Nicodemus,* raised on a
burton and deposited on the ice, and a cannon from
the armory selected because it lay closest to the
doors. The cannon was hauled over the snow by a
working party tied into man-harnesses.

Where the gun tackle would normally be affixed

to a bulwark, I had the gunner rig deadmen: crosses of timber buried in the snow, with lines made fast to them.

It then occurred to me that, in the extreme cold, the cannon might behave differently than it would in other climes. My chief concern was that it might crack in the cold. For that reason I had large fires built to either side of the test bed, a tricky matter where gunpowder was involved.

All of this special construction took time; some weeks of it, in fact. While some of *Nicodemus*'s crew members worked on that project, the remainder labored at mounting the Rodmans on their carriages and rigging them on the gun deck. Under the eye of Gunner Bellevue—a broad, square-shouldered man from Bangor, Maine—the gun crews practiced opening the ports, hauling the cannon into battery, then reversing the procedure, as each day ended much like the one before it, with a boatswain's call to sweep down and belay. Still, every day the sky grew lighter earlier and stayed light for longer.

The ship was nearly completed, as I reckoned, on the first day that I assayed to fire my cannon. I assembled my gun crew, placed the gun into battery, and had Gunner Bellevue load it carefully with a one-sixteenth charge. The cannon was laid with a gunner's protractor at forty-five degrees, and all stood well back while the charge was touched off. And so we greeted the dawn with a roar.

The cannon did not explode, and a careful inspection did not reveal any cracks. Then we, the

gun crew and I, walked the range, until the spot
where the shot fell could be found as an indentation
in the ice, and could be marked with a flag. Then we
made a second trial, with an eighth charge. Then
with a quarter charge. Then a half charge, and a full
charge, and the flags extended down the ice sheet.

"Five rounds, rapid fire," the chief said. "Then we
can try various elevations."

"Make it so."

When we came to walk downrange, the indenta-
tions in the ice from the fall of the shot all lay within
a few rods of one another.

"I'm well pleased," I said.

"Then be pleased to mount your cannon aboard
tonight." The voice, high and mild, sounded from
behind me. I had not heard the captain approach. I
whirled, and saluted.

"Sir," I said.

"Tomorrow the upper limb of the sun will cross
the horizon," the captain continued, without ac-
knowledging me. "As soon as it sinks again, at that
moment we must reach the open sea. Be good enough
to rig torpedoes the length of the necessary channel,
drilled into the ice. Bring your cannon aboard tonight."

With that he turned away; I saluted his retreating
back.

The remainder of working hours and well into
the night, as marked by the turning of the glass, we
spent in rigging the cannon on board *Nicodemus*, on
moving powder and shot into the ship's magazine,

and in drilling holes in the ice sheet ahead of her. Each hole contained a cask of powder tied with quick match to the next in line, all down the two hundred yards that extended from the smooth water of the channel, where *Nicodemus* slid forward and back like an eager horse before a race, down to the bay where the ocean rose and fell in oily swells. There, floating ice rubbed one piece against another with groaning sounds like men in torment, and keening seabirds screeched overhead.

Back in the officers' quarters, I joined my companions in packing my seabag and moving it out to the ship. I shared a stateroom aboard with Bash, Dodge, and Vincent. Our final night ashore was spent in ensuring that no wine or brandy was left behind.

After the final breakfast in the mess hall, however, when I went to make ready for freeing *Nicodemus* from the ice, Captain Sharps stopped me.

"I have another assignment for you, Johnny," he said. "We won't need guns the first day. You've got something more important to do, after you touch off the powder. Take the railway south and find a civilian, a passenger, whom we expect will accompany us on our voyages."

"At the southern terminus?"

"Indeed. A young lady, by the name of Miss Abrams. She is the daughter of an Undersecretary of War, but that is no matter. Your assignment, as important as your guns, is to ensure she is offered no insult." The captain paused and fixed me with a piercing eye. "No insult at all, from officer, man, or boy, at any time or under any circumstance."

"Sir," was all I could think to say, for all that my mind was filled with dread of how the men would reply to the idea of a female on board; the traditional "bad luck" being the least of it.

"I'm told that you have the reputation of an upright man," the captain continued.

"I strive to be one, sir."

"See to it that you continue to do so," he replied, then turned again with that abrupt way he had.

The sky grew lighter to the east-southeast. I stood with a lantern up the slope by the officers' quarters. A bundle of quick match, wrapped in paper, led from me down toward the ice sheet. The ship in her stretch of black water paced back and forth, sweeping forward to the edge of the cleared area, then sweeping back until her stern nearly touched the rearward edge. No thrashing of screw blades roiled the water below, no smoke from boilers hung above. Nor had I observed the heaps of Pennsylvania coal that were ubiquitous in other shipyards. *Nicodemus* was a mystery still.

I watched the officers and men clambering aboard, up the Jacob's ladder. The civilian workers were nowhere to be seen. The sky grew light.

From a starboard yardarm, the red powder flag broke. I watched it. The sky grew lighter still. All at once, the sun's upper limb crossed the horizon.

At that moment, *Nicodemus* stopped her restless

motion. No stir in the air, no stir in the sea. The ice made the surface of the channel appear greasy.

The sun traced a low arc, then dipped again below the horizon. Only a few minutes had, in fact, passed. The stars and stripes broke at *Nicodemus*'s mizzen top. The commissioning pennant was hauled up to the main top, and the powder flag hauled down. I touched the lantern flame to the quick match; a moment later with a roar that echoed over the base, geysers of white and grey spouted from the ice along a line continuing from the seaward side of the channel outward to the bay.

Nicodemus had been at the rearward limit of her course. Now she sprang forward and plunged into the broken ice where the explosions had lately been. She cast floes aside, she left swirling bits behind her in the water, she reached the open sea!

I turned away from the magnificent sight toward the gates, and walked to the station. The base was silent, empty of hurrying men; the energy and movement of the past days and weeks all gone. Even the preternaturally silent yard workers were nowhere in evidence. The locomotive stood there, facing south, hissing steam, hauling only the single passenger car. I mounted the carriage. The brass stove warmed the air within. Already in that brief space the sun had vanished again beneath the horizon, though the sky remained light.

No sooner had I taken a seat within the car than the locomotive started into motion, hurtling south

over the causeways that connected the Thule shipyard with its port. For two hours the abbreviated
train raced southward; and I gazed from the left-
side windows in amazement, for *Nicodemus* kept
pace with us the whole way.

*The narrative of Lieutenant
John Nevis, USN, continued.*

THE LOCOMOTIVE SLOWED AND STOPPED ALONG-
side the station building at the southern terminus. I
descended from the carriage, buttoning my coat and
drawing on my gloves. The station building was
quite deserted save for a petty officer watching over
the potbellied stove.

"Is there a young lady here, a civilian?" I asked,
after we had greeted one another in nautical fashion.

"Civilian, sir? Not that I've seen," the man replied. "*Triumph*'s in, though, came in two days ago,
might be on board there."

"I suppose she must be," I said, departed the station, and walked to the pier.

After the weeks at Thule, it seemed odd to see a
ship tied up to a wooden dock that extended from
the shore. I hailed her, received permission to come
aboard, and made my way to the captain's cabin. A
knock on the door did not bring Uncle Joe's gruff

response; rather, a girlish voice asked, "Who is it?"

"Lieutenant Nevis, ma'am," I replied. "Do I have the honor of addressing Miss Abrams?"

"You do indeed," she said with a laugh. "Please, enter."

The door swept open, and a smiling young lady gestured me in. Thule's cold saw her dressed as for a skating party in a fur-lined pelisse, and on her head a snug bonnet from which peeked a few stray ringlets of glossy black. Her eyes were similarly dark, but sparkling and fringed with thick curling lashes, and her lips were like new-picked strawberries against the creamy fairness of her complexion. She was, in short, the image of cheer and of robust good health, and I could not imagine what her role on shipboard might be.

Since she was to be in my charge on the voyage, I was gratified to see that she was no slave to fashion, and had forgone the hoops that would have made her skirts a trial to manage on shipboard. Two bandboxes and a trunk lay ready beneath the stern gallery windows.

"I heard the whistle as your train approached," she said. Her voice was a warm alto, with a trace of educated New England in its vowels. "I had ample time to pack what I'll be taking with me."

Uncle Joe Suffern chose this moment to arrive himself. "Do you have everything?" he enquired solicitously.

"I do," the young lady replied. "Save only the

flame. The lieutenant has just arrived. I am as eager to depart."

"Will you be returning by the railroad?" Uncle Joe asked me.

"No, sir," I replied. "For *Nicodemus* sailed at sunset, and will meet us here—"

Scarcely had I spoken before a lookout cried, "Boat ahoy!"

"What ship?" the lookout sang.

"Nicodemus!"

"Sunset on what day?" Captain Suffern asked, but did not wait for an answer, nor did I much feel like answering it, for I could scarcely credit the information myself.

A jolly boat was fast approaching, a lighter shape against the dark water. Before much longer, it was tied up on the opposite side of the pier, and a working party of sailors transferred Miss Abrams's luggage to the jolly boat's bottom.

"A moment," Miss Abrams said, just prior to departing the bark.

With a pair of fire tongs, she plucked out a coal from the brazier by the quarterdeck. This coal she placed inside a hollowed-out walnut shell filled with punk. The shell she closed and placed within her garments. Then, buttoning her pelisse and putting on a pair of fur-lined mittens, she preceded me down the brow and across the pier, where she allowed herself to be helped into the boat by the sailors. I took my place in the thwarts beside her and

Ensign Bash, the coxswain cast off, and the sailors gave way for the darkness.

Soon enough, the plash of oars was greeted from the darkness with the sound of the boatswain piping *mates,* then the hallo "Boat ahoy!" and the bowhook replying "Aye aye!"

The bowhook soon took hold of a lizard line and made it fast to the samson post, which brought us up against the ship's side. Then falls were attached fore and aft, and we were hoisted up, saving Miss Abrams from a clamber up a ladder, or being raised in a boatswain's chair.

As the boat came level with the rail it stopped. Miss Abrams, supported by Ensign Bash and myself, made her way to the deck. We then led her aft. The night should have been dark, neither the greater light of the day nor the lesser of the night being in the sky, yet from the north shone such a sheet of auroral flame, hanging curtains of green and red fire, that a man on the deck might have read a newspaper by their light.

Captain Sharps was waiting aft by the wheel, his breath smoking in the still air. The lurid light gave him, gave all of us, a bilious appearance.

"Miss Abrams, Captain Sharps," I began.

"Have you brought it?" the captain said to our passenger.

"Yes, I have," Miss Abrams replied.

"Come, then."

He indicated a deep bowl, standing in a tripod that rose some four feet above the deck, about where the binnacle would have been on a more ordinary ship. Miss Abrams stepped up to the bowl, withdrew from within her garments the walnut that I had seen earlier—I suppose it would have been kept next to her heart—and held it in her hand. She spoke some words aloud, though I did not understand them. They were neither Latin nor Greek; I supposed that they might be Hebrew. Then she placed the walnut to her lips, bent over, and blew through the shell. A cascade of sparks flew from the other end of the shell into the brazier, which flamed up at once with dancing flames, bright yellow in color, which gave off no smoke.

The young lady straightened. "It is done and begun," she said. "May fortune favor our venture."

"May fortune favor our venture," the captain replied. He lit a lantern from the burning bowl.

"See to it that the cook has fire," he said then. "Hot food and hot drink will cheer the men. Officers, Miss Abrams, come to my cabin, if you will."

He turned, went down the after companionway, and so to his quarters. There, candles and more lanterns were lit from the lantern he carried, bringing light and some faint semblance of cheer to the spacious room. Warmth, as yet, we had none; the air was still and frigid, and the insides of the bulkheads glittered with ice.

The captain seated himself at one end of the long table, and said, "Gentlemen, Miss Abrams, be seated, please." He picked up a flagon of wine, shook it to break the layer of ice that had formed on the top of the liquid, and poured glasses-full for everyone.

"We begin an adventure such as our nation has never seen before," he continued, when drinks were handed all round. Miss Abrams sipped at hers abstemiously, all the while gazing about with curious eyes. The cold had brought up the color in her cheeks and reddened the tip of her nose as well; a charming effect, if a distracting one. I would have to keep a close eye on the crew.

The captain continued his speech. "We stand now on a ship like no other. We have seen some little already of what she can do; before long I daresay we will see more. The war at sea in the current struggle for our nation is a simple one. The damned Rebels send out raiders against our commerce at the same time as their own merchants purpose to trade with England, seeking to gain money and supplies for the fight, and seeking also to bring John Bull into the war on their side. The Federal Navy, for its part, in order to prevent Confederate trade with England and forestall the alliance, has blockaded the Southern ports.

"Our mission is simple, gentlemen. We are to destroy the blockade runners and commerce raiders wherever we may find them, and prevent the Rebels from lifting the blockade." He turned his eyes to our fair passenger. "Miss Abrams—have you brought anything for us?"

"Yes, Captain," Miss Abrams said. "I bear letters from the Navy Department, from the Secretary of

War, from President Lincoln, and from my father. Here they are, sir."

From the same hiding place within her garments where she had held the fire, Miss Abrams withdrew a sheaf of envelopes and one scroll, sealed with pale wax.

" 'Woe, woe, woe, to the creatures of the earth,' " Captain Sharps said with a smile, and broke the seal on the scroll. It disturbed me to hear the Book of Revelations quoted in such a casual, almost humorous, fashion, but it was not my place to question the captain's wit, and I therefore held my peace. Blasphemy on naval vessels is the common talk of sailors, however much one might wish otherwise.

He perused the scroll, then laid it aside. "That's well," he commented in a low tone. Then he lifted the next letter, this one in a standard envelope. The contents of this were all in a cipher, which the captain worked out as we watched, with the aid of a pencil, a sheet of foolscap, and a bronze wheel inscribed with letters and numbers.

"Most serious news," he said when he was done and had read the information. "Our agents in England inform us that the Rebels' plans are farther advanced than we thought. We will not have the luxury of sea trials, nor yet of a shakedown cruise. Make preparations to get underway; we sail at once for England."

Charts were brought forth, a track east by south laid in, and the countless other details seen to. In the midst of this, Miss Abrams and her luggage were stowed in a cabin just forward of the captain's, and notable for its size, second only to the captain's cabin as well as for having a commode leading directly to the waterline.

"Heavy seas and that'll be interesting," Ensign Bash commented, and I had to agree. The thought came to my mind, though, that this vessel had been built from the keel up to have a female on board.

What else was missing came to me at that moment. Ships are ruled by time, and time is set by bells: Every half hour, the quartermaster of the watch should turn the glass and strike the bell. When men eat, when they sleep, when they work, when they stand watch, all are governed by the bells. And yet, since coming aboard *Nicodemus* I had not heard the note of a single bell.

I went up on deck, and walked the length of it under the roiling, aurora-colored sky. No bell. Every ship gets a bell on the day of its christening; when a ship is taken from service its bell is removed. The bell is the soul of the ship.

This ship had no bell. I supposed, therefore . . . "Has this vessel been christened yet?" I asked Lieutenant Dodge, whom I found on the quarterdeck.

In reply he merely laughed. "Never went down the ways, never had a bottle smashed on her bows— so no, I don't think you could say that she was."

At this moment, the captain emerged from aft, a rolled chart in his hand.

"Mr. Dodge," he said. "You will take the deck.

Get underway. I won't be unhappy to leave this cold and dark behind."

"Sir," Dodge replied with a salute.

Soon enough, the boatswain was piping *All Hands*. Miss Abrams stood by her bowl of fire, which had now died down to embers. She fed in small sticks, each one setting loose a cloud of sparks, making me worry about fire amidst the tarred line and pitch-caulked seams of our vessel. No one else seemed to be concerned.

"Take in the sea anchor," the boatswain cried.

"Take her in," echoed the man by the starboard cathead. "Haul on the tripping line."

A party of men hand-over-handed the light line in, the cork anchor buoy bobbing closer and closer. Then, when the canvas funnel of the sea anchor was by the cathead, the boatswain called, "Take in the riding hawser," and the foredeck hands put a turn around the capstan and brought her home. The sea anchor came up on deck, and was flattened, coiled, and stowed below on the spar deck to dry.

"Underway," Dodge said to the quartermaster standing by. "Mark the time." Then, to the helmsman, "Rudder midships."

The helmsman stood motionless, gripping his wheel. Dodge turned to the man standing by the trick wheel, mounted fore and aft to the port-hand side of the quarterdeck: "Ahead dead slow."

The man turned the small wheel forward, and slipped a loop of line about a spoke to keep it from moving farther forward or back. I became aware of a corresponding change in the ship's motion, as the sparks that had been drifting straight upward now began to blow back aft before winking out.

Seas struck us on the bow, making the ship shudder with each impact. Above us, the stars wheeled against the yards as the ship turned. Polaris was behind us now.

"If we get out of this haze we'll steer by the stars," Lieutenant Dodge said. "Until then, eyes aft and keep the wake straight."

With those words we departed the rocky coast. Clouds were coming from out of the west, eating up the stars and the fire of the aurora in the north. The lights of the brig *Triumph* faded astern.

"Boatswain," Dodge said to the petty officer who stood by him, "see to it that the lookouts are rotated frequently. It would be a sorry thing if any of them got frostbite, after all this."

"Sir," the boatswain's mate replied, and walked forward.

I approached Miss Abrams.

"Miss," I began.

"You may call me Columbia," she said. "For it is my name; nor need you be so formal with me. I am not in the Naval service."

"I should not wish to be too familiar with you, Miss Columbia," said I. "The captain has placed your comfort and safety in my care, and I take my obligations seriously."

"I believe you do," she said, with a smile. "I believe you do indeed."

"I own that I cannot see the reason for putting a gently raised young lady into conditions of such hardship and possible danger."

"My duties concern this," Columbia said, pointing to the flames.

I touched the tripod with its burning bowl. It was firmly bolted to the deck. "Then you are in some sense a Vestal?"

She dimpled. "Not in so many words, but, yes. You could call me that."

My heart sank within me. Nothing I had learned at the Naval Academy had mentioned Vestals on board Navy ships.

"Shall I see you to your quarters, Miss? It's dreadfully cold."

She smiled again. "Yes, Mr. Nevis, you may."

Emboldened by her earlier comments, and by the fact that she was a civilian, I said, "You may call me John."

"The beloved apostle," she said. "I might have known."

With that she retired to her quarters. I remained without until I heard her set the bolt in her door, then made my way to my own berth.

I was awakened by a man holding a lantern.

"Sir, you're on watch next," he said.

I swung from my bed. I had gone to sleep all standing, from the cold, and so did not need to spend much time in dressing. Lieutenant Vincent had the deck on my arrival. The sky was a transparent blue, the last stars fading before dawn. *Nicodemus* was rolling lightly in a moderate groundswell on the starboard beam, the wind fresh from the starboard quarter. I looked astern, and saw the wake straight as an arrow to the horizon.

"We're making ten knots, steady east by south," Lieutenant Vincent said. "Underway for England."

"This is odd," I said, looking about. Miss Abrams's bowl of fire was still burning, a canvas sack of kindling hanging beside it. "To go without sail or steam. I scarce know what's left for us to do."

"Fire gets low, stoke it," Vincent said. "Not much else. Haven't seen another craft all night. Lot of birds—terns, mostly."

"Think we'll have heavy weather soon?" I asked, looking away to the east, where the sun was rising through a blood-red mist.

"Likely enough."

"I'm ready to relieve you," I said.

"I'm ready to be relieved."

"I relieve you," I said, and saluted.

Vincent returned my salute. "I stand relieved." Then, in louder tones, he sang out: "On the quarterdeck, this is Lieutenant Vincent. Lieutenant Nevis has the deck."

"On the quarterdeck, this is Lieutenant Nevis, I have the deck," I said in equally loud tones.

The necessary ritual completed, I turned to the messenger of the watch standing by. "Please inform the captain, observed sunrise. And bring me a mug of coffee on your return."

"The captain is aware of sunrise," Sharps said.

Again, I had not witnessed his approach. He stood bareheaded beside me. "Today it is my intention to see what this ship can do. Mr. Nevis, please give me the deck. Turn out your gunners. I greatly fear that their skills have grown rusty, too long in dry dock."

"Captain has the deck!" I sang out, then went forward to find Gunner Bellevue.

From the private diary
of Miss Columbia Abrams.

MARCH 22ND, 1863

ONE DEVELOPMENT I SHOULD ACKNOWLEDGE, AT least here in the pages of this journal where none can read my more indecorous thoughts without first breaking my private shorthand: I find that I take a great deal of enjoyment in contemplating the large number of handsome young men that the United States Navy has seen fit to attract. Even Captain Sharps is not altogether unpleasant to look upon, although I must admit he is not young, and the demands of his metaphysical studies combine with the burdens of rank to make him seem cold and distant.

The junior officers, on the other hand, are all most attractive, and not at all cold, though they are, of course, perfectly gentlemanlike in every way. I will own that I have not yet succeeded in remembering all of their names. After spending four years at Hadley, where the only male creatures we saw from one week to the next were the chaplain and the gardener—both of them near to their biblical three score and ten, if not already past it—I find the presence of so many vigorous representatives of the stronger sex to be most distracting.

The only one of them I can put a name to in my mind, as yet, is Lieutenant Nevis, who met me in advance of the rest of *Nicodemus*'s crew, when he came to fetch me off the *Triumph*. He is quite fine-looking in his uniform, being of a lean rather than a stocky build, yet free of the gawky quality that mars the appearance of so many tall men. His eyes are a pleasing shade of bluish grey and his hair is light brown and gently waving; his complexion is somewhat weathered but not, at the moment, tanned, from which I infer that he has spent much time of late either ashore or in the prolonged sunless winter of these northern latitudes.

He is, I think, a purely *naval* man, and I believe all the other officers are the same, saving only Captain Sharps, whose scientific and metaphysical studies made this enterprise possible. If the captain seems harsh and unbending, it is no wonder; even my own small schooling is enough to let me guess at what sort of trials and privations he must have endured in order to attain his present level of knowledge.

A piercing whistle sounds, and I must put my

journal aside and inquire as to what it signifies. The days here are ruled by the notes of the boatswain's call, and I am determined to master the language of them before we reach England.

*From the private diary
of Miss Columbia Abrams.*

TODAY I SAW FOR THE FIRST TIME THE TRUE NA-
ture of the force that gives life and motion to *Nicodemus*. The experience has provided me with much to
think about.

The day began with one of the ship's boys knocking at the door of my cabin. "Captain Sharps's compliments, Miss Abrams," he said, "and he requests
that you robe yourself and meet him in the lazaret."

I would never have answered the door had I not
been fully dressed to begin with, and surely the captain knew it. I reasoned, therefore, that he meant me
to wear the garments he had supplied for me, which
had come aboard *Nicodemus* in a bandbox kept separate from all my other luggage. My work aboard ship,
he had given me to understand, would be such that a
fatal pollution might arise from contact with my usual

clothing—this, in spite of the rigorous and minute inspection to which all of my garments had been subjected at the start of my journey.

I will admit in these pages that I never considered how many parts of my wardrobe were steel or iron until I had to remove every trace of those unwanted metals. No steel in my corset stays, or my hairpins, or even the shanks of my buttons—it was nothing less than providential that I had already resolved to give up my hoops for shipboard wear.

The robe Captain Sharps gave me is made of unbleached wool, hand spun and handwoven. A single seamless garment, it wraps around the body after the fashion of Greek or Roman antiquity, and is fastened in place with heavy bronze pins. The costume is not unpleasant to look upon, though it is not something I could ever wear in public. Not only does it leave my arms and shoulders completely bare, but I am strictly enjoined against wearing anything whatsoever beneath it.

Quite the wanton, you would think. And so I might be, except that the homespun wool scratches most dreadfully against my skin. If I am ever to be a wanton, I shall insist upon wearing nothing harsher than cambric or lawn.

But I wander far from my story. I bade the messenger wait outside my cabin until I was ready, then made haste to shed my everyday clothing and don the ritual robe. When that was accomplished, I stepped out of my shoes and let down my hair—even as a schoolgirl, I knew that it was always best to approach metaphysical or spiritual workings with unbound hair and bare feet—before flinging a hooded cloak over it all, to shield me from both vulgar glances and the cold sea air.

Wantons, I am certain, are never troubled by goose-flesh, either.

I see that I am wandering again. I must discipline myself to go onward.

When I was ready, I opened the cabin door and allowed the boy—who had been waiting most patiently this whole while—to escort me to the lazaret, where Captain Sharps was expecting me. I was half fearful that the captain might also have robed himself for the occasion in the antique manner (it would not, I think, have draped well on his lanky frame), but to my relief he wore his customary uniform.

"Miss Abrams," he said.

"Captain," said I.

"It's time you had a formal introduction to your chief charge and concern aboard *Nicodemus*."

"I am eager to do that very thing," I replied.

"Then follow me," he said, and I did so, going forward through a narrow companionway to a locked door.

The door was guarded by two sturdy specimens from the ship's company of Marines. Captain Sharps said, "Miss Abrams has authorization to enter this space at any hour of the day or night," and they said,

"Yes, sir," after which the captain took out a ring of bronze keys of most unusual design, and worked one of them in the lock.

I heard the lock click over. The captain said, "Your cape, Miss Abrams, before we enter." I took it off and gave it to the nearer of the two Marines—who was gazing very fixedly at the opposite bulkhead and not at my bare neck and shoulders at all, which was gentlemanly of him.

Then Captain Sharps opened the door, and I was admitted to a room full of light. The blue-white illumination that suffused every corner of the space had no source that I could at first determine. No lamps or lanterns hung there—if such a glow could ever have come from a living flame—and no light came into the room from the world outside; there was only the room itself and the object in its center.

How can I describe what I saw? Mere enumeration of form and dimension—that it stood even taller than Captain Sharps; that he and I could not have encircled it with our arms outstretched to their limits; that it was made up of concentric rings and bands, with a solid globe at the heart of it—cannot suffice. If I add that it was, in itself, the source of the room's light, perhaps I am coming closer to setting forth the nature of the marvel, for every edge and curve of it was limned in cold blue fire.

I thought of Moses, and the bush that burned but

was not consumed. Before I could chide myself for the blasphemy, I heard the voice of Captain Sharps speaking at my elbow.

"You see before you the heart of *Nicodemus*."

I took a step closer to the device. Above it, a curious network of hempen ropes stretched from one side of the room to the other, with blocks and sheaves and iron weights suspended from them, to what purpose I could not fathom. The heart itself—

"It's made of wood," I said. I was surprised; I had thought at first that such a coldly glowing structure would have to be made of glass or metal.

"It was carved to my design from a single block of chestnut," he said. "No one living has laid hand on it since the day that it was finished."

"How did it come here, then?" I asked. "Such a heavy thing as this could not be moved by mere wishing—and I see that it is both taller and wider than the door through which we entered."

Captain Sharps laughed. "You are an observant young woman, Miss Abrams. Every living soul who has touched the heart since its completion has worn gloves, and the ship was constructed around it."

"How does it work? I don't understand the purpose of all the ropes and weights."

"It is not necessary that you understand," he said; "but in brief, the presence of iron, brought closer to the heart or taken farther away from it, can either goad the ship into action or bid it rest. For this reason, it is critical that the heart be cared for properly."

"You say that it is to be my responsibility," I said. "But I have no gloves. Not dressed as I am now—which is also by your design."

I will own that I spoke somewhat impertinently, especially to such a stern and forbidding man as the captain. I was emboldened, however, by the knowledge that I was necessary both to his project and to the ship. So long as I was not disrespectful or disobedient to him in public, I judged that he would not chastise me overmuch for light words uttered in private.

"The heart of *Nicodemus* is an armillary sphere carved out of a single piece of living wood," the captain said. "All of its parts must move freely, without drag or crack or warping, if it is to function at the peak of its efficiency. It must be attended to on a daily basis in the sea's harsh environment, and to do so it must endure the touch of a human hand. My researches indicate that a pure virgin is the one least likely to disrupt workings of the heart."

I looked at the glowing sphere. "What am I to do now?"

"On this first occasion, merely lay your hands upon it and introduce yourself. More will come later."

I was unsure, but I did not want the captain to see my doubts. I stepped up to the great sphere and, after a moment's hesitation, laid my hands flat against the wood of the outermost ring. It felt warm under my skin, as though it had stood all day out in the sun.

I wet my lips. "*Nicodemus*," I said. "I am Columbia Abrams, and I have come all this way from Washington to make your acquaintance."

From the private diary
of Miss Columbia Abrams.

MARCH 30TH, 1863

I SPOKE WITH LIEUTENANT NEVIS TODAY. HE HAS, I am told, been charged by his captain with being my keeper on shipboard. He glares most ferociously at any of the sailors who happen to let their eyes linger on me for longer than he considers appropriate; and I once overheard him giving a severe dressing-down to a man on one of his gun crews, on the grounds that the man had spoken of me with insufficient respect.

The other officers aboard *Nicodemus* are not so zealous on my behalf as Mr. Nevis. Neither are they so personable, so I suppose it all evens out in the end. Mr. Dodge, the ship's second in command, is a taciturn man, at least in the presence of women, and burdened as well by the necessity of dealing with the captain on a daily basis. Lieutenant Cromwell bears the title of ship's engineer, and I believe has some degree of metaphysical knowledge as well; he and the captain are the only men permitted to enter the ship's engine room (or what would be the engine room, if *Nicodemus* had engines of the ordinary sort). Lieutenant Vincent is the ship's navigator, and a Marylander, from the port of Baltimore. His loyalty to the Union is unshakeable—indeed, he is estranged from his family because of it—but he makes no secret of caring little for the cause of Abolition, and I cannot approve of such disregard for the most serious moral question of our time. Mr. Bash, the supply officer, is an ensign scarcely older than I am myself, and the monastic nature of his schooling and of life at sea has rendered him scarcely able to converse with a woman at all.

Captain Sharps I must speak with daily, by his own requirement, in order that he may cross-examine me on the regular performance of my shipboard duties. Some people might find such close attention flattering, but not I. Tending to the ship's fire is but a housekeeper's task, for all its significance, and my part in caring for the heart of *Nicodemus* is much the same. Were it not for the sense of awareness and welcome that I felt upon first touching the great sphere, the daily work of cleaning all of its interlocking and moving parts and anointing them with protective oils would seem of little more consequence than maintaining a cumbersome piece of furniture. Even the ritual chants and invocations which I spent so much time learning all these months past, and with which I am enjoined to accompany the work, are not meant to benefit the ship directly, but to foster my connection with it against the day when we go together into battle.

Beyond my work on his ship's behalf, Captain Sharps has, I think, no interest in me at all. *Nicodemus* itself is warmer to me, and more forthcoming.

Lieutenant Nevis, unlike some of his shipmates, is neither too forward nor too shy in my presence—I must remember to inquire if he has sisters at home, that he came by this ease with those of my sex—and the nature of his duties all but obliges him to engage me in conversation. Today I asked him how he came to be serving aboard *Nicodemus* (for he is by nature the most straightforward and unmystical of men—quite unlike the captain in that respect). He told me that he came of a seafaring family and had received his commission before the start of the war, and that since then he has gone wherever those in authority have seen fit to send him.

"Then you did not volunteer for this?" I asked.

"The project was a secret one," he replied. "I could scarcely volunteer outright. But no one constrained me to join the naval service, and all the rest follows from that."

"Nevertheless, you seem happy to be here."

"The prospect of action cheers me. I didn't join the Navy so that when war came I could sit at a desk ashore and dabble in an inkwell."

"You are very brave," I said. "The . . . 'prospect of action,' as you call it, frightens me sometimes."

"It's nothing to be ashamed of. Women were never meant to be in the thick of battle, and it speaks well of you that you volunteered, when so many of my own sex have not." He paused, looking concerned. "You *did* volunteer, I hope. To conscript a young woman such as yourself would be an infamous act."

I reassured him that my service was indeed voluntary, and our conversation turned to other things.

*From the private diary
of Miss Columbia Abrams.*

APRIL 2ND, 1863

IT HAS BEEN SCARCELY A WEEK AND A HALF SINCE I first came aboard this ship, and already the cold northern latitudes begin to recede into memory. To-day I packed away my woolens and flannels in exchange for garments of linen or cotton cloth, saving only the robes I must wear on my visits to the heart of *Nicodemus*—twice each day, at morning and evening, by Captain Sharps's orders. I now have my own key to the locked room, so that I may attend to my duties without needing to disturb him.

When first I received my instructions, I expected to find the regular visits tedious. Long hours spent cleaning and anointing the armillary sphere and intoning what Captain Sharps has assured me are vitally necessary chants are no substitute for friendly conversation and the company of like minds. (And while I would not place Captain Sharps in that congenial category, *Nicodemus*'s junior officers—particularly Lieutenant Nevis!—are another matter).

I certainly did not anticipate finding, dare I say, a kindred spirit in *Nicodemus* itself. But from the first instance when I laid my hand on the sphere and introduced myself to the ship, I have felt a personality—a presence—within this vessel's wooden heart. Today I spoke of it, cautiously, to Captain Sharps, after he had finished with his habitual questions about the progress of my daily work.

"When I told *Nicodemus* my name," I said, "it was as if I experienced . . . recognition, perhaps. Or a greeting."

"I'm not surprised," he said. "Every named vessel has an indwelling spirit of sorts. It is for this reason that the common sailors speak of ships as living creatures."

It was not just the common sailors, I knew that much. I had heard Lieutenant Nevis and his fellow officers speak so as well. But I did not think Captain Sharps was the sort of man who would easily bear contradiction. So I said only, "Are they in error, then, to speak thus?"

"It is not a natural spirit," he said, "but rather an acquired one, compounded from the traces of vital essence left by all those who have worked or sailed aboard a particular ship, imbued with coherence and identity through the giving of a name."

"Much as some old houses take on the imprint of

the generations who have lived in them?" I ventured. Captain Sharps favored me with an approving nod.

"Just so."

But despite the fact that I cast my eyes modestly downward, as a young woman may when she is praised by her elders for having arrived at a proper conclusion, I do not think that it is—entirely—so. I have lived in more than one old house, and sailed aboard the *Triumph* on my journey north, and in none of those places did I feel the same awareness and sense of connection as I did when I introduced myself to the heart, as Captain Sharps described it, of *Nicodemus*.

I told myself that the matter bore thinking on. To the captain, I said no more on the subject; however, I have resolved to speak privately with Mr. Nevis, who has had experience with ships of all sorts. Captain Sharps has much learning in mystic and metaphysical matters, and has a great store of both occult and general knowledge; but ships and the sea are only a lesser portion of what he knows—whereas John Nevis has made them the whole of his study.

I have determined that my best opportunity to consult with Lieutenant Nevis will come during one of the night watches, when speaking quietly will not be taken for "murmuring"—which is, I gather, frowned upon as a sign of discontent. All that remains is to wait for a cloudless night, when a young woman such as myself might plausibly venture to ask a gallant officer questions about the art of navigating by the stars . . . and about the nature of ships and their souls.

* * *

Later—

Tonight I succeeded in having private conversation with Lieutenant Nevis. I waited until the sun had descended below the western horizon, and he stood alone and somewhat aloof on the quarterdeck. I approached him with some trepidation, for while we had talked before, this would mark the first time I had ventured to speak even elliptically of the heart of *Nicodemus* with anyone save the captain.

We conversed for a little while about trivial things and, more soberly, about the course of the war—we had heard no news, of course, since leaving Thule, and were not likely to have any until reaching England—before I felt able to raise the question for which I had sought him out.

"You seafaring men talk of ships as though they were persons," I said.

"True," he said. "We do speak in that fashion."

"But do you honestly believe that it is so—or is it merely a customary turn of speech?"

"I would not admit to any heathen superstition," he said. His manner appeared uncomfortable, in the way that some practical men have when forced to talk about philosophical matters. "But two ships can be made in the same yard to the same plan by the same shipwrights, and one will be a handy sailer who brings her crews and captains nothing but good fortune, and the other will be a luckless man-killer until the day she goes to the breakers."

I pondered this for a moment and decided to come at the question from another angle. "Captain Sharps would have me believe that a ship's soul is but an artificial thing, a kind of patchwork made from scraps of vitality left behind by sailors and shipbuilders. Do you agree?"

"No," he said at once. "There would be no need to christen a ship and give her a name if her spirit were not real and true."

"I thought you might say that," I told him. "Tell me something else, then—"

"If I can."

"*Nicodemus* was built in secret, and in a strange shipyard. Do you know whether or not she had a proper christening?"

"She had her name already when I arrived," he said. "But I have not heard of any ceremonies when it was given."

*The narrative of Lieutenant
John Nevis, USN, continued.*

ON THE MORNING OF THE FIFTH OF APRIL, AT TWO
bells of the forenoon watch (though as we had no
ship's bell, the signal was given by the boatswain
piping *Mates* at every turn of the glass), Captain
Sharps appeared on the quarterdeck. He asked me
if I would be so kind as to ask Miss Abrams to attend him in his cabin. I complied with his request,
conveying his compliments. Upon escorting her
there, the captain said to me, "Johnny, my lad, see to
your guns. I hope to see action before sunset."

We were sailing at that time in a deserted ocean,
not having seen any sail for nigh onto a week. Nor
was one in the offing even then, but I at once did as
the captain bade. Not just naval discipline lent me
vigor, but a certain keenness in the captain's eye
which suggested he knew more than he said.

The guns, of course, were perfectly in order. The
lines and fittings endured the gunner's inspection,
and mine as well. Subsequently, I had powder and

shot brought up as if for an afternoon's gunnery practice; the men thought nothing of it, for we had practiced often. I was pleased with their efforts.

The watch changed. The wardroom noonday meal was not tense, but rather more alert than was common, from which I judged that Captain Sharps had hinted of action to more than me alone. All this time the captain had remained closeted with Miss Abrams, taking his meal with her.

At one bell of the afternoon watch, the captain and Miss Abrams emerged from his cabin—he looking keenly about, his lips compressed into a thin line, and she looking somewhat pale but resolute nonetheless. Miss Abrams at once made her way below. Captain Sharps, meanwhile, climbed into the mizzen stays, holding a spyglass in his hand. From that point of vantage, he surveyed the horizon away to the south without a word. He spent perhaps ten minutes thus before descending to the quarterdeck, whereupon he spoke to me again.

"Load both sides," he said, then retreated for a second time to his cabin. He emerged a few minutes later wearing a long robe of blue velvet like a cassock, with a matching half-cape trimmed in ermine.

Captains have their little eccentricities, and much leeway is given to them in matters of uniform at sea. Captain Sharps's unusual garb was in no wise the strangest example of such that I had ever encountered. I saw that in addition to the blue velvet cassock, he held a gold ring tied to a thread, hanging from the fingers of his right hand. This he observed closely, giving orders to the helm as he did so.

"Come right. Steady as you go."

At that moment Miss Abrams again came on deck, but dressed this time in a loose woolen smock of Attic design, held in place at her shoulders with bronze pins. The sea breeze pressed the fabric to her form in a most distracting manner, and I was forced to speak sharply to a sailor who had turned from his duties to gawk.

She was barefoot, and the loose white fabric revealed her ankles as it whipped about her. She did not speak but took a place on the forward part of the quarterdeck, in the center of the inlaid ring of bronze that I had noticed on first coming aboard *Nicodemus*. Standing as if rooted to the deck, she lifted her arms and pulled out the pins from her hair. The rich dark mass of it fell about her shoulders in a flood, freeing the stray curls and tendrils to lift gently in the wind.

Then she raised her arms above her head and stood unmoving, facing forward. Her eyes were not focused on the ship, nor on the horizon; although she appeared to look forward, at the same time her gaze seemed to be turned inward.

"Speed," cried Sharps, and the helmsman turned the trick wheel.

The ship leapt forward, so rapidly that I stumbled before regaining my balance. Miss Abrams did not move.

"Faster!"

This time the ship's acceleration was smoother. The waves split before us, curling up in twin jets of spray, glittering in the sun.

"Faster!"

Now the bow of *Nicodemus* began to lift out of the water, and the wind of our passage blew straight back. Miss Abrams's hair streamed out behind her, and the rush of air pressed the fabric of her shift against her body from neck to ankles, revealing all.

"Eyes forward," I ordered the gun crews.

A moment later there came a cry from aloft that seized and fixed any attention that might still have been turned in Miss Abrams's direction. "Sail ho!"

"Port side," Sharps said. "Run out the guns." Then he turned his face upward and called out, "Do you mark her?"

"Aye," came the cry down from aloft. "She flies Rebel colors."

Sharps grinned in a lupine manner. "Very well."

He placed the golden pendulum in a slit-pocket in his cassock. Then he resumed his place in the rigging, and gave a series of orders to the helm.

As he did so, I could make out against the horizon the top of a mast, then three masts, then sails: a ship-rigged vessel, making way under full sail.

"Faster!" Captain Sharps sang out, and again we accelerated. I would not venture a guess at our rate of speed, save that it was both unnatural and tremendous.

We altered course to starboard, and my crew stood to their guns. *Nicodemus* was steady in the ocean, not rolling, but with a tremor in her timbers, pitched up by the bow. White spray rose above the main deck to either side by the head and was whipped aft by the wind; the sea boiled astern of us. In less time than I would have believed possible, the Confederate Stars and Bars was visible on the approaching ship's main truck even without a glass.

"On my command, rolling broadside," I said, and the gunner replied, "Rolling broadside, aye."

What astonishment our sudden and furious appearance might have awakened in the other vessel, I could only imagine. Despite serving on *Nicodemus* since departure from Thule and seeing something of her capability, I myself could hardly credit it.

We passed under the Rebel's starboard quarter, and pulled our broadside, gun by gun, as we passed her sternpost. At the speed we were making, I regret that our accuracy was poor despite the close range.

"Shift your side!" I cried.

My gun crews hopped nimbly to the starboard side, where the guns already lay loaded, and ran them out. As we did so, Captain Sharps shouted "Shift your rudder!" and *Nicodemus* came about, the deck inclining, as best I could estimate, some forty-five degrees to starboard. At such an extreme angle, it was all I could do to keep my feet.

We came about, steadied, our keel level, and commenced another pass up the side of the Rebel ship. Again we fired a rolling broadside, this time with better effect, for I observed hits on the Rebel's hull on her starboard quarter, yet at this angle her rudderpost was out of sight and so unscathed.

"Shift your side, reload!" I called out to the gunners.

Again we came about, this time in a hard left turn. The deck heeled to port so steeply that again I had to hold on to a railing. Miss Abrams did not move, nor seek to hold on to anything, but instead stood as if rooted, her hands still lifted skyward above her head. We reloaded the guns swiftly, but now, as we fired, the Rebel brought a single gun to bear, and as we passed up her starboard side, she fired.

The shot struck us by the bow.

"He's one hell of a gunner, to have hit us," I heard one of my men say to another, in the brief instant before *Nicodemus* came to a sudden halt. All her forward motion ceased absolutely and her bow sank into the sea, so that she was taking on green water where an instant before had been white spray. All those on the deck were thrown forward, and I lost my footing.

Then *Nicodemus* began to spin around—the axis being a point on the port bow—as if she were a screw auger attempting to bore her way into the ocean. We kicked out waves about us, as the after portion of the ship traveled sideways through the water in a motion wholly unnatural. A cry of dismay rose from the crew.

"Widdershins!" Captain Sharps said. "This cannot continue. Carpenter forward! Find out where we're hit. Report my damage."

"Aye, Captain."

The carpenter sprinted forward, past the gun crews. Once at the ship's rail, he leaned far out to inspect the hull.

Meanwhile, the dizzying motion of the ship continued. Spray flew all around us, and shadows chased across the deck as the sun appeared to spin around us overhead. Through all this, the Rebel ship had not left us. Rather, she was taking in sail and running out her cannon.

"To the guns!" I cried. Perhaps in this emergency it was not the most helpful thing to do, but if we were to be in a sea fight, I could not endure the idea that we would not return fire.

The carpenter left the rail and came back to the quarterdeck. "Seems to be a ball lodged in the planking, Cap'n," he reported. "In the strake just above the devil, close along the stempost."

"Dislodge it," Captain Sharps said. Very shortly, in response to his order, the boatswain and two of his mates had rigged a chair and were lowering the carpenter with his bag of tools over the side near the prow, a line tied around his waist, while the captain observed their endeavors with approval.

Then he turned to me. "Sir, you are not aboard as an idler! Put a hot fire upon that Rebel pirate."

"Sir, the order has already been given." Discipline forbade that I protest the insult further, but I felt a rush of angry blood burning my features nonetheless. "I wish to inquire if you have special instructions as to whether to aim for their hull, or for their rigging, sir."

"As you will, and trouble me no further."

I turned away, and returned to the waist where the gunner stood. "Fire at will, at any target that presents," I said.

He saluted and I turned my attention to the guns. The men were acting as they had drilled, and I was pleased thereby. What pleased me less was the prospect of the Rebel, for she was taking in her courses and running out more guns than I had expected a merchant to possess. I feared that we had chanced upon a commerce raider, and now the Rebel, sensing our vulnerability, would seek our destruction.

For vulnerable we were indeed. The motion of the ship was even more unnatural than the incredible speed that the past weeks had in part trained me to disregard. As we pivoted about our stem, we rolled on our port beam ends and churned the sea into a maelstrom, with our starboard battery pitched at the sky while the port battery pointed to the sea. I doubted that any aiming was possible.

"Unship outboard trucks to starboard," I said. The effect was to lower the muzzles of the guns to a more serviceable elevation.

The Rebel had come about and was approaching on a reach taking the weather gauge.

"Take what you can," I told my lead gunner.

Soon enough, the Rebel swung into view again, and a ragged fire commenced from our starboard side. I could not mark the fall of shot, for as we swung a more amazing sight came to my attention. We were rapidly driving in a circle, and the Rebel was passing astern of us. To my shock and horror, at that moment I saw Miss Abrams place her hands upon the bronze pins that fastened the shoulders of her shift and, with a deliberate gesture, remove them. In an instant her garment tumbled about her feet, revealing her in a state of absolute nature.

I turned away and commanded loudly to my crew, "All hands, eyes forward!"

The men were struggling with the guns to bring them back into battery, for without the outboard trucks the guns did not move easily; in addition they were hauling the gun carriages up the pitched slope of the deck. Even so, a few of the men were stealing glances aft at Miss Abrams despite my order. I remonstrated with them to see to their duty.

The Rebel was passing up our port side, and at this moment loosed a broadside upon us. Shot fell to either side, but by a miracle none touched either hull or rigging.

"Load, and fire at will," I exhorted the gun crews, and they did so readily. If nothing else, we made a good deal of smoke and noise.

Then all at once, with a lurch, the deck heeled over and once again became level. *Nicodemus* leapt forward, and the boatswain's mates hauled lustily on their lines to pull the carpenter, wet and choking, from the sea into which he had been thrown.

Immediately thereafter, Captain Sharps placed the Rebel's bow broad on our port beam, where we could bring our whole side to bear but they could fire only their chasers. After that first hit, no other ball from the Rebel ship came close, and our accuracy and weight of fire soon unshipped their foremast. Shortly afterward they struck their colors.

Now came another event worthy of mention. I commanded my crews to cease fire, and made my way aft, averting my eyes outboard for the sake of Miss Abrams's modesty as I passed. A life spent at sea gives little opportunity for experience in metaphysical matters. I had heard it said, as one might hear about the professional mysteries of astronomers or engineers, that certain projects exist for which the practitioner should have as little clothing as possible separating himself from the elements; but I had never thought to find myself depending upon such for my safety in battle.

The captain regarded me coldly. "Lieutenant," he said, "is there a problem with the guns, that we have stopped firing upon the Rebels?"

"No, sir," I said; and added, by way of—I thought—unnecessary explanation, "They have struck."

"Fire, and continue to fire," said Captain Sharps.

"Aim for the hull, and do not cease until you have rendered her in a sinking condition."

For the second time since the start of the engagement, I found myself struggling to repress an angry response. "Sir, the law of the sea—"

"Is what I say it is," Captain Sharps said. "Will you obey my command, sir?"

I saluted, went forward, and directed the fire until the Rebel was dismasted entirely, and going down by the head. Again I stilled the guns, ordered the men to see to them, and returned aft. Miss Abrams had by that time regained her decency—such as it was in the thin fabric of her shift—and stood facing the captain with her chin raised and her cheeks high-colored.

Captain Sharps, for his part, appeared equally incensed. "Madam, when I call upon you to provide protection for this vessel, protection is what I expect."

Miss Abrams's eyes flashed. "How many of your men are injured, Captain? How many killed?"

"It is not sufficient," the captain said. "*Nicodemus* herself must remain unscathed."

"So she is, Captain," said Miss Abrams, and until then I had not thought that one so fair could speak with such cold anger, "and so she shall remain. Good day, sir."

With that word, she turned upon her bare heel and went below in the direction of her cabin.

We turned east, then, and sailed straight away.

The sinking hulk of the Rebel vessel became a dot on the horizon astern, then vanished. The sun set.

Captain Sharps did not join the officers at the evening meal.

From the private diary
of Miss Columbia Abrams.

NICODEMUS GROWS INCREASINGLY UNHAPPY that we have traveled such a long way from the far northern regions. I have said nothing to Captain Sharps about this; he has his orders, after all, and his plans as well, and it is not my place to speak against them unasked. If he desires at some point to know the temper of the ship, then I will tell him what I know. He at least would believe me if I spoke; most of the other officers aboard would likely attribute it all to womanish fantasy.

But I am the one who spends hours out of every day in the locked and guarded room that houses the great armillary sphere; I am the one who speaks and sings to it; and I am the one who listens to it in return. And I say that it is no fantasy on my part that makes the heart of *Nicodemus* warm beneath my hand, and no fantasy that the touch conveys to me impressions of feelings and images I recognize at once as not being of my own making. I have seen the vast white reaches of the polar snows, with the aurora hanging in the night sky above them in a waterfall of light; I have felt what it is to travel on the etheric planes, free of the sullen earth below and unimpeded by any physical form; I have touched in memory the comforting presence of others of my kind.

In memory only, for I am—for *Nicodemus* is—lonely and alone.

I recall the day that I first became aware of the ship's heart as a living entity. It happened after we had defeated and sunk the Confederate raider. Before we saw battle, I had been afraid that my courage would fail me—that I would hide in fear of death by rifle ball or cannon fire, or that I would prove unable to abandon modesty for the sake of a greater good. But I kept to my battle station and did my duty, even when *Nicodemus* spun and bucked in the ocean like a demented whirligig; and I found myself afterward poised on such a high point of self-confidence that I was able to face down Captain Sharps when he sought to cast aspersions upon my work.

But all such peaks must have their valleys, and once the exultation faded I was restless and dispirited. I had no appetite for my dinner—though, in the immediate aftermath of battle, I had felt ravenous enough to devour anything that might have been set before me—and slumber eluded me.

After a long period of restless thought, I decided that I needed to seek out Lieutenant Nevis for conversation. We had talked before about my need to go with *Nicodemus* into battle, if not about the precise form that such a duty would take, and he had proved himself at that time to have a sympathetic ear. Also, I thought it likely that he could speak from experience, and say whether or not my descent into low spirits was a common thing.

I rose from my bunk and dressed myself in my everyday garments. Throwing on my cloak for a barrier against the night air, I ventured up on deck, to where Lieutenant Nevis was standing watch. He was aware of my approach, I could tell, but did not turn and speak to me, only continued gazing out across the starlit ocean.

Perhaps I should have spoken to him then. Not until much later did I consider that his silence was born, perhaps, of a certain awkwardness (for he had seen me that day in a state which under any other circumstances would have been most improper). But his aloof demeanor, as I then thought it, intimidated me as the thunder of battle had not, and I could not bear the thought of a rebuff.

I turned away; but instead of returning to my cabin, I made my way to the locked room that housed the heart of *Nicodemus*. The Marines on guard let me pass without question—had not the captain himself said that I was to be allowed admittance at any time of the day or night?—and I stepped into the blue-white glow and closed the door firmly behind me.

"Ah, *Nicodemus*," I said. I approached the great

armillary sphere and leaned my forehead against it. As always, the polished wood felt warm against my skin, and what I had on first acquaintance thought odd, I now found comforting. "I should have come and thanked you earlier."

When I spoke, I seemed to feel an increase of warmth in the wood where I leaned against it. Warmth, and a sense of comfort—well, I had come here looking for something of the sort, and had hoped to find it in quiet communion with the ship's indwelling spirit, whatever that spirit's nature might actually be.

"I hadn't known you could move so quickly through the water," I said. "Lieutenant Nevis talked about seeing you outpace a steam engine, but hearing of something is not the same as *knowing* it."

Saying the lieutenant's name aloud caused me to experience a sudden pang—I had counted upon his sympathy more than I had known—and the sensations of warmth and comfort coming out to me from the heart of *Nicodemus* perceptibly increased. I was filled in the instant with what the poet would surely have termed a wild surmise.

"*Nicodemus*," I said. "You can hear me. You *know* me."

Again I felt the comforting touch, this time with a surge of happiness riding behind it. An image came into my mind—the ship's deck, seen from a vantage point somewhere far above. White water streamed away from her like the plumage of some great bird, and sunlight sparked off the polished brass of her guns. The figures of men hurried about her decks, seeming no larger than tin soldiers to my hovering eye—and among those figures, another, with loosened hair and robed in white.

"That's—is that how I look to you?"

A sense of affirmation swept over me, and I knew that it was so. Our communication had no words, at least not on the part of *Nicodemus*, but I was certain now that it was communication just the same.

"And that tall officer standing by the guns is Lieutenant Nevis. He's a good man, *Nicodemus*, but I fear he is displeased with me."

Kindness and disbelief flowed outward from the heart of the ship . . . I think I wept a little, and shook my head.

"It's true. Because of what I had to do when we were fighting the Confederate raider. I don't know if he respects me any longer."

Disbelief again, stronger this time, and images of the battle—of Lieutenant Nevis exhorting his gun crews to action, with all his attention fixed on the work. *Nicodemus* clearly approved of John Nevis, and was concerned that I not think ill of him, or fear that he thought ill of me.

"His manner has changed toward me," I said. It was odd, perhaps, to be talking about such things with a bodiless and inarticulate spirit, but ever since coming aboard I had suffered from the lack of a confidante. I knew that *Nicodemus* would keep my secrets. "He doesn't know enough to understand how important it can be that nothing get in the way of the transmission of vital elemental energies. I could explain to him that I am merely a conduit, or a link in the chain, but I fear that he would resist the understanding still. Or if he did not, he would nevertheless contrive to blame the captain for ordering me to work in that fashion. Which would not be entirely fair. The captain is much more learned than I in metaphysical matters; if he could carry out this work himself, and spare everyone the trouble of having a lone female aboard ship, I'm sure he would have done so."

The image of Lieutenant Nevis faded, only to be replaced in my consciousness by the features of Captain Sharps, seen not at a distance but with a clear and terrible closeness. The sky behind him was not the cloudswept blue of these southern latitudes, but a deep and arctic black. I had never seen the captain looking thus—his hair long and wild, his eyes burning, his cheeks gaunt with privation. It had to be either some disordered fantasy of my own mind, or a memory belonging to *Nicodemus*.

"You have seen him like this?"

Agreement. And the captain's hands, a sword in one and a thurible of burning incense in the other. Circles within circles drawing endlessly inward. His lips moved, but I could not hear the words.

"What—when did this happen? And where?"

Time and space, alas, proved concepts too abstract for the still wordless communication between myself and *Nicodemus*. The image faded, and I sensed only a roiling frustration on the part of my newfound friend—frustration, and the certainty that while *Nicodemus* might be fond of me, and might approve of Lieutenant Nevis, the ship we all sailed on hated the man who sailed her.

From the private diary
of Miss Columbia Abrams.

APRIL 10TH, 1863

TONIGHT I WAS A GUEST AT DINNER IN THE OFFI-cers' wardroom. This came as a welcome change from dining alone in my cabin, which until now has been the usual case. I am inclined to suspect that once having a female aboard ship ceased to be a novelty, the younger officers began to find my presence to have a dampening effect upon their conversation.

Captain Sharps was not with us at first; I was given to understand by those at the table that he frequently dines apart from his fellow officers.

"Not a sociable man, our captain," Mr. Vincent said. "And not one much given to friendly talk. There were times in Thule, while *Nicodemus* was still abuilding, when we would scarcely hear a word out of him from one day to the next, except to give an order now and then to the shipwrights."

"And a da—... dashed peculiar lot they were, too," put in young Mr. Bash, the supply officer. "Made the Old Man look talkative. You could ask them a simple question—'Did the captain come by here this morning?' or 'Have you seen my spyglass?'—and not get a word out of them by way of answer. They'd just stand there and look at you until you went away."

"Surely it demonstrated spirit," I said. "At least, of a sort. Not many workers would be so daring."

"Skilled laborers willing to stay in a place like Thule are not easily found," said Lieutenant Nevis, "and are well paid and well treated accordingly. Whereas we poor Naval men must go where the government tells us, and bear up under the insolence of civilians."

"I must protest," I said, laughing a little. "I for one am not insolent, I hope."

"Not in the least," he assured me; and Mr. Bash said, "Those yardbirds in Thule would have needed to learn to speak before they could be insolent. Dealing with them was like talking to dumb cattle, and none of us had the gift for it. Except for the captain—and Mr. Dodge has a story to tell about *that*."

"Now you rouse my curiosity," I said. "There's no denying that *Nicodemus* is an extraordinary ship; but I came aboard too late to see what kind of men it took to build her. I would very much like to hear Mr. Dodge's tale."

"So would I," said Lieutenant Nevis, when Mr. Dodge at first appeared reluctant. "As the last arrived of the ship's complement—with the exception of

Miss Abrams—I have missed hearing any number
of interesting tales, and what I saw of the workers in
Thule intrigued me."

"Very well, then," said Mr. Dodge. "You shall hear
it, and make of it what you will."

He then began to tell the following story, which I
have transcribed here in this diary as faithfully as
my memory allows, both as to substance and to general idiom:

You're asking me about the yard workers in Thule,
the ones who built this ship. Well. That's a question
with two answers: the easy one, that I'd be willing to
write down on paper and sign my name to for anyone
set in authority over me, and the other one, that I
wouldn't be telling if we weren't all here on board
ship together. They're both true—you can let your
conscience rest on that score. I haven't made a false
official statement yet in my career, and this voyage
isn't the time I'd pick to start.

My honest report on the Thule yard workers, if
anybody asked me for one, would say that they were
quiet and industrious, not given to gossip or to muti-
nous talk, and moderate in their habits. I could also
say that they were good craftsmen, willing to labor
for long hours without complaint. And every word of
it would have been true. It just wouldn't be the whole
story, not by a long stretch.

I can recall my first sight of them, when I was but
newly arrived in Thule myself, and the ship was only
stacks of lumber under tarpaulins on the ice; I re-

member the day well—it was in October, the same day as when the sun went down below the horizon to begin our six months' night. Captain Sharps had arrived the day before, and had made himself known to the future officers of *Nicodemus.*

He came on the *Triumph,* which left him here and departed again in a hurry, and I would have sworn that he traveled alone. But when by the regular turning of the sandglass we knew that morning had come (though the sky was no lighter outside than before), and I went to begin my day's labor, I saw two long lines of workmen drawn up by the waterside for inspection.

They were an odd lot, standing there in the light of the gas lamps: tall and sturdy, but with a stoop-shouldered look to them that made them appear shorter to the casual eye. They wore heavy winter garments of drab-colored cloth, not so identical as to be called a uniform, but near enough to make me wonder if they'd all been hired from the same village somewhere. A few of them had unworn faces and a few others had wrinkled ones, but all of them had long beards and long hair down past their collars. I'm from Pennsylvania, and we have our share of Old Believers there, of one kind and another; I thought at first that the new yard workers were more of the same.

Captain Sharps walked all the way down one of their lines, and all the way up the other, nodding to himself and smiling a smile. Now would have been the time to address the new workers with some kind of encouraging speech, to make them welcome in their new home and hearten them for the long winter night, but he never spoke to them at all, only murmured "Excellent, excellent" under his breath and kept on smiling.

"Captain Sharps, sir," I ventured to say, when he had made his complete inspection. "Do you wish me to take charge of the workmen?"

He brought his gaze back to me. "That won't be necessary, Mr. Dodge," he said. "They know their own business well enough."

It was true. The men broke ranks as I watched, and went to work without needing instruction. They worked all that day, and every day after that—even on Sundays, which made me think that they might not be Old Believers of the Pennsylvania sort at all. Every morning I would see them going to work in the lamplight, and every evening would see them returning. They had quarters all their own, a long, low barracks of a building, that was off limits to all others. And day by day—though it was all one long night, if you disregarded the calendar and went by the sky outside—the ship they were making for us grew.

I wouldn't have known anything more about them, though, if it hadn't been for the snowstorm. It blew up one morning while I was at my desk devising the ship's watch, quarter, and station bill, for *Nicodemus*'s ordinary seamen had begun to arrive. By the time I was done and ready to go back to my quarters for the night, the air outside was so thick with falling snow that the lamps could do no more than make blurry glowing patches in the dark.

I thought at first of staying in my office until the storm ended—I've heard as many stories as the next man about what happens to those who get lost in a midwinter wilderness—but the idea lost its appeal the more I pondered. The level of coal in the scuttle had fallen quite low, and would not be replenished until the next workday, which meant that I would have a chilly night once the fire burned out. Moreover, my office, such as it was, contained only a desk and a straight-backed wooden chair; the cot in my quarters, while narrow, was luxury itself by comparison. Also, I was hungry, and there was no food or drink where I was.

So, foolishly, I put on my gear and headed back to my quarters, navigating from one dimly seen lamp to another. And just as someone not quite as foolish might have predicted, I soon lost my way. I followed what I thought was the correct line of lamps all the way out to its end, only to find nothing there. Retracing my footsteps didn't help; I hadn't thought to count the lampposts the first time, and what I thought was the main road only ran out once more to end in darkness.

I don't know how long I might have wandered from light to light, or what might have become of me there. But when two long lines of yard workers came out of the driving snow not far from where I stood, I know that my heart leapt up to see them. They moved with purpose and surety, as men might who knew their

way and were not lost; and I was happy to attach myself to the end of their silent parade. If I were fortunate, they would pass by my quarters on the way; and
even if my good fortune did not extend so far, I could
pass the night with them and return to my proper
place when the storm blew itself out.

I was only half lucky. The next building we came
to was the workers' own dark barracks. The first
man in the line opened the door, and two by two
they all entered, with me coming last. Then the man
who had opened the door closed it again, and we
were left in the dark.

I heard the thumping and rustling noises that you
would expect to hear when a number of men are getting ready for bed—though all of it was done in
complete silence, and without the faintest spark of
light. After a time, I grew tired of standing and waiting, and began feeling my way forward, taking it slow
and careful as a man might who didn't know the barracks and its furnishings well enough to go about
with his eyes closed. Before long, I came up against
the hard wooden edge of a bunk, catching myself a
nasty bang on the shin and swearing aloud from the
surprise of it.

"Begging your pardon," I said afterward, thinking
surely I must have given the bunk's occupant a start,
but no one else spoke; "I'm cast up here by the storm,
d' y' see, and in need of a place to sleep for the night.
So if you could shift over and make room alongside
for me, I'd be mightily grateful."

Still no one said anything. So—taking silence for

consent—I felt my way into the bunk that I had col-
lided with only moments before. The sleeper had not
shifted far enough to give me much room, but the
bunk was still better than the cold floor, or my office
desk and chair, and here at least there was a blanket.

I don't know how much time passed by while I lay
next to my unmoving bunkmate and waited for the
chill of the air outside to leave my extremities. At
length, however, I began to realize that I was not
growing warmer, as by rights I should have been
with another body lying next to mine. A horrid suspicion rose up in me at the thought—who was to say
that the man beside me had not returned exhausted
from his labors only to expire, silently, in his bunk?

I reached out a trembling hand and groped in the
darkness until my fingers met the side of my bedfel-
low's neck, and followed the tendons down to the
place where a pulse should have leapt beneath my
fingers.

And felt nothing.

I moved my hand further—found his lips in the
wiry tangle of his beard—held my fingers a little
away from them and waited for the warm puff of an
outgoing breath—

Again, I felt nothing.

I rolled out of the bunk and scrambled to my feet.
"Wake up! Whoever is in charge here—wake up
and fetch a light! You have a man here lying dead!
Awake!"

No one responded or struck a light. The darkness
and silence remained as absolute as before.

I stumbled away from the bunk where I had been lying, and found another by falling against it. I grabbed the occupant by the shoulder and shook him.

"Wake up!" I cried. "He's not breathing—wake up!"

But the body under my hand was as cold, as stiff and unmoving as the one I had touched before. In a sudden spasm of terror, I flung myself away, wanting nothing more than to find the doorway and flee into the open air. Even the chance of freezing to death in the snowstorm seemed preferable to remaining a second longer in the dark barracks with its unmoving occupants.

I stumbled backward over some unseen item, for the interior of that barracks was as dark as a cave in the bowels of the earth. I lay on the cold floor, and as I lay there, the door as I suppose opened, and a brilliant light, painful to look on, approached. I sat up, and there was Captain Sharps, holding his hand aloft and holding therein, as I supposed, a prismatic lantern. His features were heavily shadowed and harsh, and the breath steamed from his mouth.

"Rise," he said. "Come forth. This is no place for you."

I did so, and followed, in a waking swoon. I awoke the next morning, lying still dressed in my bunk in the officers' quarters, with the memory of the previous evening's events already fading like a dream.

But this thing alone I remembered clearly, that I saw in the workers' barracks by the actinic light in the captain's hand: a score of men, motionless, eyes open as they lay on wooden shelves, their cheeks glittering with ice.

Mr. Dodge finished his tale, and for a little while silence filled the wardroom. Lieutenant Nevis and I may have been the only ones present who had not heard the story before, but clearly all the others—including Mr. Dodge himself—were almost as strongly affected by hearing it retold.

What might have happened next, had the conversation been left to pursue its natural course, I cannot tell. Of a sudden the wardroom door flew open and Captain Sharps stood on the threshold. He had a terrible frown, and spoke to us in a voice like thunder.

"What debauchery is this?" he demanded. "Miss Abrams is a gently reared girl, and not an audience for your lurid tales."

Lieutenant Nevis paled a little with anger. As my designated guardian and attendant aboard *Nicodemus*, he must have felt the insult keenly; and when I heard how stiffly he replied, "This is no debauchery, sir. Miss Abrams is a guest of the wardroom, and has been treated with every respect," I feared that he might choose to take mortal offense.

I hastened to add my part. "I assure you, Captain—Mr. Nevis and his friends have been all that is courteous. Mr. Dodge enlivened the evening with narrative at my request."

The captain turned his angry gaze onto me instead.

"Then have a mind to your virtue, Miss Abrams, for it is of vital import. Henceforward, you dine either in your cabin alone, or with me."

I grew angry myself then, that he should think I cared so little for my own honor, and would have answered him roundly indeed, save that Lieutenant Nevis pressed his foot hard against mine under the table, and I remembered in time the deference that was owed to a captain aboard his own ship.

"As you wish, Captain," I said, with all the grace I could muster. But I could not rouse my enthusiasm to stay longer in the wardroom, with Captain Sharps glowering at me as though I might become a fallen woman at any minute, and shortly thereafter made my excuses and retired to my cabin.

*The narrative of Lieutenant
John Nevis, USN, continued.*

WE HOISTED SAIL FOR THE FIRST TIME DURING
the voyage for the passage up the Bristol Channel to
Portsmouth. The change from our previous rapid
and almost effortless passage through the water was
remarkable—how soon do we accustom ourselves
to things which should remain marvelous!—but
England was known to be rife with Confederate
spies, and it would not do to have our regular mode
of progress observed. Once at Portsmouth, we de-
clined a pilot, instead anchoring in the stream.

Captain Sharps desired me to accompany him
and Miss Abrams ashore, and we departed in the
longboat to fleet landing. Mr. Bash was boat officer,
and six sailors rowed. As we stepped upon the pier,
"Shove off, await my signal" was the whole of the
instruction that the captain gave to Bash.

There was to be no liberty for the crew in Portsmouth, a situation that had produced some grumbling before the mast, as Gunner Bellevue informed

me the day before as we inspected the carriages.

"No help for it," I replied. "It is the captain's express desire that the nature and description of this vessel should not become the common talk of the taverns."

Once ashore, the captain, Miss Abrams, and I presented ourselves to the port captain. The formalities having been observed, we made our journey to London by way of the Portsmouth Direct Line of the London and Southwestern Railway. From the railway station, we went by public carriage to Mansfield Street, Portland Place, and the residence of the United States Minister to England.

Miss Abrams was dressed most modestly for the journey, and professed herself glad to be on dry land for a time, though she admitted that the jolting motion of the railway car was in truth not so smooth as *Nicodemus*'s normal movement through the water. Outside of such exchanges, however, our conversation was strained. I could scarcely bring myself to look Miss Abrams in the eye, for fear that my features should betray how vivid remained the memory of all that I had seen so shortly before. In any case, a railway carriage was no place for idle banter, far less a hired coach where the driver could overhear. Captain Sharps, for his part, kept his thoughts to himself.

Once in the minister's residence, we sat in an anteroom awaiting that gentleman's summons. The westering sun cast its light through the windows onto the far wall. A servant brought tea and cakes, of which Miss Abrams and I partook, though Captain Sharps did not. Nor did he sit for long, but paced the room restlessly.

At length a different man entered the room: not a servant, but appearing in a well-cut suit in the British fashion. "Mr. Adams begs your indulgence," he said, "and craves your forgiveness for the delay. I am Chalmers; the word of your arrival only lately reached the minister. Will you accompany me?"

Captain Sharps inclined his head, and offered his arm to Miss Abrams. Chalmers led, the captain followed, and I brought up the rear. Up a staircase, down a hall, and into a study we went. There the minister waited, together with another man, in civilian attire, and Lieutenant-Commander Randall, the naval attaché, in uniform. I had heard that he was an efficient and active officer. A glance now at his eager expression confirmed that report.

Mr. Adams said to Chalmers, "Thank you. Now go to the end of the hall and make sure no one approaches within twenty feet of this room. We have some matters to discuss."

With that, Chalmers departed. Mr. Adams took a seat behind his desk and begged us all to be seated and make ourselves comfortable. "There's sherry on the sideboard," he said. "Feel free to refresh yourselves if you feel the need. We can be informal here."

Captain Sharps again inclined his head, but made no move in the direction of the sideboard. I determined to follow the captain's lead and not indulge unless he did; and Miss Adams, of course, said nothing. The civilian was not so reticent, for he at once strode to the sideboard and poured himself a generous portion.

We made introductions all around, the civilian being the only one not to speak. Mr. Adams filled in that gap. "The gentleman standing by the globe"—here he indicated the civilian gentleman—"is Mr. Armstrong. He is a confidential agent of ours, although not a citizen of our land. Sometimes," he added, sitting back, "that can be a useful thing. Nevertheless, you may speak as freely before him as you can before me or Randall."

Captain Sharps did not appear reassured, but the civilian spoke then, the burr of the Highlands of Scotland making his words almost unintelligible. "Ye need tell me no secrets, Captain," he began. "I know most of the business already. Rather, I'll be telling you secrets. As for who and what I am, know that I studied at Melrose Abbey, and am myself a seafaring man."

"What secrets do you mean, sir?" Sharps asked.

"We have had a report that may interest you keenly," Armstrong said. "A recent letter to Paris, concerning a certain Confederate vessel, was intercepted, read, copied, translated, and lies here in my pocket."

With that he pulled out a number of sheets of folded foolscap, closely written in an impeccable hand, and gave them to Captain Sharps, who read through them while the clock on the wall ticked loudly in the silence. When he was done, Sharps gave the papers to Miss Abrams, who after reading them, handed them on to me.

"There's more," Mr. Adams said, after we had all seen the letter. "The United States Army has had a report from the Caribbean region, which I believe is pertinent."

He withdrew a portfolio from his desk drawer, and took out a thick bundle of papers, which the captain, Miss Abrams, and I likewise read in turn. The content of these pages was even more unsettling than that of the letter of Captain Jean-Claude Lesquignard to the French Ministre de la Marine.

From the field journal of Captain Edward Bartlett, USA. Recorded in a personal short-hand adapted from the Pitman method.

MAY 15TH, 1862

IN CONTINUANCE OF MY INVESTIGATIONS INTO the rumor of William Walker's experimental cannon foundry, I have after much effort located a guide willing to take me upcountry to San Anselmo.

My official story—that I represent commercial interests in the CSA desirous of gauging the suitability of Mr. Walker's Nicaragua for *latifundia* on the Southern model—did well enough for me here in Managua, where my dealings were largely with representatives of the landowning class. Outside of Managua, however, its utility proved more limited, and I was forced, in the end, to deliberately let slip my Yankee origins. I used the tale that I was an agent of Mr. Cornelius Vanderbilt, and that my interest lay not in farming but in railroad investment, at some future date when the restraining hand of war should be lifted from the commerce of nations. Mr. Walker's animosity toward Mr. Vanderbilt, after the latter's unsuccessful attempt to unseat him from the presidency of Nicaragua, is well known, and my efforts to draw a veil of dissimulation over my supposed association with him are readily understood.

My guide, Tomás, is not likely to be numbered among Mr. Walker's admirers in any case. While his mother is an Indian woman of sufficient skill as a cook to find employment in the kitchens of the local rich, his father was African, brought to Nicaragua in slavery by one of Walker's *filibusteros*.

Tomorrow morning we will set out for San Anselmo. My false purpose for being in this country should allow me to come within a few miles of whatever it is that Walker has been building. Speculation is rife, though the theory that it is a foundry for cannon of a new and especially deadly design continues to my mind the most likely.

MAY 28TH, 1862

The weather continues intemperately hot. Tomás and I make progress but slowly toward our goal. Much time is taken up by the necessity of maintaining my dual disguise. I am required to observe and to make notes, and to be seen doing so, in a manner consonant with my presumed role as a representative of Confederate agricultural interests. At the same time, I must be visibly—but not *unduly* visibly—at work scouting out the local terrain with an eye toward its suitability for railroad travel. All this, of course, without revealing the actual purpose of my investigations. If nothing else, my work to date should insure that any person taxed with the responsibility for observing my movements will not find it unusual if I veer off at some point in an unexpected direction.

My peregrinations have, however, given me a fair idea of the location of Walker's cannon foundry, if such it proves to be. Every person whom I have asked about suitable land—whether for rails or for farming—has included in his reply a list of places I should at all costs avoid. These places vary, of course, according to the story I have told them, but when put down on the maps that I have with me they display a startling unanimity of opinion concerning San Anselmo.

"Very bad people there, *señor*," says one. "They will break your legs and rob you blind."

"Fever," says another. "No *gringo* can live out a year in that place."

"The ground there is completely unsuitable." This, from an educated man, the *patrón* of the village of Los Torres, who had studied, so he said, at Salamanca during his youth. We spoke in English, both for discretion's sake and because he desired the practice. "Whether for farming or for . . . other things." And he gave me a look, as if to let me know that he had penetrated my Confederate disguise.

Then he spoke again, more slowly. "None of my people will venture there, whatever the threat or encouragement. Nor will I; in this matter I take my guidance from them. *Los brujos*—do you know the word, *señor?* . . ."

I nodded. "The witches," I said. "The midwives and cunning-men who live among the people. We have them also."

"*Bien.* You will understand me, then, when I warn you that *los brujos de Los Torres* say that San Anselmo is cursed."

MAY 29TH, 1862

Rain today, from early afternoon until near sunset. Tomás informs me that we are entering the time of year when heavy rains are of daily occurrence. The inclement weather will make our travel slower and more difficult. At the same time it will serve to obscure my interest in certain places where neither of the persons I am presumed to be would ever venture.

Tomás and I start out tomorrow for the supposedly accursed San Anselmo. I have told the *patrón* of Los Torres that I am turning back to Managua with the advent of the rainy season. If he suspects that I am lying, he at least has the courtesy to feign belief.

JUNE 5TH, 1862

Rain continues. The intermittent periods of sunshine serve only to make the atmosphere more oppressive, as our selves and the landscape alike steam in the increasing heat. My only comfort lies in the knowledge that we are drawing steadily nearer to San Anselmo. The sooner we are there, the sooner I can complete my business in this country and make the fiction I gave the *patrón* into truth.

JUNE 6TH, 1862

Still more rain. We have penetrated well into the territory surrounding San Anselmo, and I judge that one more day will bring me into close range of Walker's establishment, whatever it may be. I find the idea of a cannon foundry ever more unlikely; I saw nothing in Managua, or on the road afterward, to suggest that anything so bulky as the necessary materials or the finished armaments was moving either into or out of the country.

I have determined to leave Tomás here at our camp and make the remaining portion of the journey alone. While I am confident in my ability to observe and remain unseen, the possibility of discovery always exists, and I would not have him come to grief through his association with me.

JUNE 13TH, 1862

The *brujos* of Los Torres were right.

San Anselmo is accursed.

But I run ahead of myself. I chose to make my final approach to San Anselmo on foot, since I expected concealment at some point to be necessary, and neither my horse nor Tomás's donkey would lend themselves readily to such expedients. I had not expected, at the time, to find that Walker's clandestine base of operations was not in San Anselmo proper, but rather on the very shore of Lake Nicaragua—though in retrospect I should have done, since the Rio San Juan is navigable from Lake Nicaragua all the way to the sea.

Accordingly, I found myself, at the end of yet another afternoon of torrential rain, lurking on the outskirts of San Anselmo in a state of sodden misery. My discovery that the goal I had sought for so long, and in such discomfort, contained nothing resembling a cannon foundry or any other warlike structure—or, indeed, anything at all beyond a cantina, an empty church, and a few small houses, all built of the native stone and weathered by the passage of time—left me more than half convinced that I had been chasing a chimera all along. It was in this state of extreme and, I see now, reckless disgruntlement that I determined to abandon subterfuge and seek out whatever lodgings might be had.

Behind the obscuring veil of steady rain, a yellow glow of lantern light shone out through the chinks of the cantina's shuttered windows. To the cantina, accordingly, I bent my steps.

The door was closed, but swung open when I pushed it. The room inside held more people than I had expected. A place the size of San Anselmo should not have possessed close to a score of drunkards so confirmed that they would absent themselves from their own hearths on such a night as this. On the heels of that thought, as I cast my gaze over the clusters of rudely dressed men who sat at the rough wooden tables, there came another: These were not the good people of San Anselmo; rather, they were laborers from Walker's mysterious establishment.

I determined on the instant that my tale of being a surveyor in Vanderbilt's employ would not suit in this company. My identity as a representative of Southern agrarian interests was not much better. So far as I could determine, the soil of San Anselmo was fit for raising little save mud, and that in quantity. I would have to be a guest of the *patrón* of Los Torres, I decided, a subterfuge which had the advantage of having lately been true. Should anyone inquire further, I would claim to have been distracted from my agricultural surveys by an amateur naturalist's curiosity about the surrounding forests.

Though it was flimsy in my judgment, the story passed muster—the drinkers in the cantina seemed more than willing to believe that I had lost my way while searching for rare plant specimens in the pouring rain. I should stay the night, they said, eat and drink and let my wet clothes dry as much as they could, and in the morning someone would put me on the right path again.

The meal they gave me was stew from the common pot, corn and squash and pork. In my tired state I found it delicious, and ate hungrily. Yet I was not so unsuspecting as to accept without question the glass of strong spirits—rum, by the smell—that the owner of the cantina pressed upon me afterward, for he poured it from a separate bottle previously untouched, and a scent I did not recognize underlay the more familiar aroma of the rum. In the dim lantern light I was able to feign drinking the liquor slowly, as if savoring it like fine brandy, though in fact most of it went discreetly onto the packed-earth floor.

After a time, when the glass was empty, I rose from the table with an unsteady stance—since I deemed some variety of sleeping drops to be the most likely additive to the doctored rum—and, yawning hugely, inquired of the host where I should spend the night.

The cantina, I was assured, had a room upstairs, and the host would be most honored if I should choose to sleep in it.

I yawned again, for the sake of my deception. "The honor will be all mine," I said. "Lead on."

The upstairs room held a cot and a washbasin, and little more. The latch on the door was a crude wooden toggle that could have been lifted by an industrious schoolboy with a dull butter knife. I remained uncertain whether the purpose of the sleeping drops was to render me an unconscious, and therefore easy, victim, or to prevent my discovery of something that would happen in the night.

I bade my host good-night with yet another vast and artificial yawn, and allowed myself to collapse heavily on the bed, in what I hoped was a convincing imitation of a man under the influence of a soporific drug. I was determined, however, to remain awake, if for no other reason than to learn what it was that had been intended.

I lay for some time unmoving, doing my best to imitate the profound sleep and stertorous breathing of one who is drugged. My efforts were rewarded when heavy footsteps paused for a moment outside my door, and a rough voice asked, in Spanish, "Is he sleeping?"

"Like the dead," said the innkeeper.

"Good. We have work to do. Alecto needs men."

"Hungry bitch."

"It's true, she has a boundless appetite. *El Señor* wants two from San Anselmo this time."

"*Two?*" The innkeeper's hoarse whisper was full of outrage. "By God, he asks too much. San Anselmo cannot afford to lose so many."

"Then spare one and take the *gringo* instead."

"There will be trouble if we do."

"No. Men die in the jungle every day, especially curious *gringos*. 'He stepped upon a viper and it bit him above the boot; we are very sorry, *señor*, but the weather was warm and we had to bury him before he began to rot.' "

I trembled, then, at the choice that lay before me:

abandon my feigned sleep, despite having overheard what the sleeping drops had been intended to conceal; or continue as I had been, and let myself be taken, unresisting, to that Alecto who was a hungry devourer of men. But the choice, I realized in an instant, was in truth no choice at all. If I revealed myself to be awake, the tavern keeper and his companion would doubtless insure my continued silence by the most permanent means possible, and I would perish here in San Anselmo without ever learning the truth about William Walker's secret enterprise.

Better, then, if I must die, at least to die with my curiosity assuaged—and if my captors believed me to be drugged insensible, then I might yet retain some hope of escape and freedom.

CARRYING OUT MY PLAN, HOWEVER, PROVED more difficult than I had initially anticipated. Without further ado, the tavern keeper and his companion entered my room, seized me by ankles and shoulders as though I were no more than a sack of potatoes, and bore me ungently outside between them. I was hard put to maintain my resolve in the face of such treatment; fortunately, I was not transported in this manner for very long. A donkey and cart waited in the dark outside, and it was into this rough conveyance that I was unceremoniously deposited.

The cart rattled into motion—a form of progress scarcely more comfortable than before—with my two captors walking alongside. They conversed in low voices as they went along, but spoke no more of

Alecto or of what might be intended for the two men she had apparently demanded tonight from San Anselmo. I dared, then, to open my eyelids to more than mere slits for the first time since hearing the tavern keeper's footsteps outside my room, and to take stock as best I could of my physical situation.

As I had already suspected, I was not alone in the cart, but shared it with the second portion of Alecto's human tribute. He had not been taken unresisting; his hands and feet were bound, and the moonlight that shone down from gaps in the wind-torn clouds showed that his face was swollen and marked with dark clots of earth or blood.

For my own part, I was keenly aware of my good fortune in being neither injured nor bound. A sleeping draught meant to keep me insensate until morning had apparently been deemed security enough. Greatly though my conscience pained me, I did not venture to make known my relative freedom, or even my conscious state, to the other man. I was determined to hoard whatever slender advantage I currently possessed until such time as I had discovered at least some part of what I had journeyed so far, and put myself at such hazard, in order to see.

The journey to the shore of Lake Nicaragua was not overlong, but uncomfortable enough to seem a great deal longer. The necessity of continuing to feign a drugged stupor meant that I could not change position to brace myself against the cart's dips and lurches on the track. The resultant accumulation of cuts and bruises at least provided me with some distraction from morbid fantasies. A peculiar curiosity, such as I suspect a bird feels when facing a serpent, compelled me to see the drama to its last act.

At the lake shore, the bound man and I were manhandled, without ceremony, into a rough wooden boat, perhaps a dugout canoe (the requirement that I once more shut my eyes to escape detection prevented me from observing it more closely). Our captors joined us, and rowed us for some distance out into the lake. Although I still dared not open my eyes, the use of my other senses was not lost to me. I soon heard, quite clearly over the plashing of the oars and the heavy breathing of the oarsmen, the unmistakable sounds of a large ship lying at anchor.

So, then, I reasoned, *Alecto*, the "hungry bitch" of whom the tavern keeper had spoken so resentfully, was a ship. William Walker's secret project in aid of the Rebel states, that had so incensed Cornelius Vanderbilt when rumors of it came to his ears, was no more than a common raider or blockade runner, augmenting her crew by impressment among the local population. The truth of the matter would reassure those in Washington who tended to regard Walker—after his improbable and continued success against all efforts to unseat him—as a mystical savant of the highest order. It certainly reassured me, since it would appear that I faced at worst an involuntary enlistment in the Confederate naval service.

Thus, at any rate, my thoughts ran, as our boat drew ever closer to the anchored *Alecto*. Underneath those thoughts, however, ran an increasing current of disquiet that would not be denied—for my bound companion lay whimpering and sobbing in abject fear, and the wind blowing toward us from *Alecto* carried with it the scent of blood and more-than-tropic corruption.

I dared slit my eyes open again. Our boat drew nearer to the looming bulk of *Alecto* without regard for my presentiments. I gathered from the low-voiced converse of the oarsmen that their duties would end when they had brought myself and my companion alongside, and wondered how I could maintain my pretense of drugged sleep if we were expected to attain *Alecto's* deck under our own power.

We were, as it happened, hauled aboard in nets like cargo—an experience I wish neither to dwell on nor to repeat—and deposited all in a heap upon the deck. The smell of blood was stronger here, a heavy slaughterhouse stink, even though the wooden planks where I lay were worn smooth with scrubbing; and the air was filled with the buzzing of flies.

I decided to risk opening my eyes fully for long enough to look around. I had feared that my apparent return to consciousness would attract the notice of one or more of my captors—thus making my eventual escape difficult, if not impossible—but I need not have worried. I was only one prisoner out of perhaps a dozen lying bound or otherwise subdued, under the guard of crew members armed with clubs and machetes. So long as I neither moved nor made a sound, my open eyes were unlikely to draw anyone's notice.

The wooden planks onto which I had been so unceremoniously dumped were as clean as holystone
and sand could make them. *Alecto* might be every
vile thing the innkeeper in San Anselmo had said of
her, but someone took pride in her nonetheless. I did
not have to look far to see who it might be. Half a
dozen men stood surveying crew and captives from
the vantage point of *Alecto*'s quarterdeck, but only
one of them wore the uniform and insignia of a Confederate naval captain.

The men standing with him on the quarterdeck
were five in number. The four largest and most muscular were dressed in the everyday garb of the laboring classes. The fifth man, seen in the intermittent
moonlight, presented an appearance at once outlandish and sinister. His thick dark hair was matted and
clumped into spikes, the studs that pierced his ear-
lobes were the size of silver dollars, and the knife
tucked under his belt had a blade almost as long as a
man's forearm, made of some dark substance. In retrospect, I believe it to have been chipped and flaked
obsidian, but at the time I could say only that it was
not metal. He stood next to a lump of some dark material—in the moonlight, I could not tell whether it
was wood or stone—a little more than waist high,
and about the size of a small table. Though its four
corner edges were roughly square, its upper surface
was oddly humped, rather than level.

The Confederate officer spoke to this man in flu-
ent, if accented, Spanish. "You have what you need;
get on with it."

"Of course." The other man's accent was not a local one, but I thought that perhaps I might have heard something similar to it while traveling in northern Mexico before the war. He indicated a position close by the humped table. "You will stand there, please. As before, *Capitán*."

The officer moved to the new position as instructed, although his countenance and demeanor made it plain that he had no relish for doing so. His attitude did not surprise me. I am a landsman, not a sailor, but even so, by virtue of my profession I have some knowledge of what is and what is not done on shipboard. Sailing vessels have their own inherent nature, and seamen in general mislike trifling with it; they feel, or so I have gathered, that it is in most cases best to leave such things alone, and trust to the more dependable mysteries of wind and water.

As soon as the captain had been repositioned to his satisfaction, the man at the table pulled the black knife from his belt and slashed it across his empty palm. He stretched out his bleeding hand above the table, the knife still gripped in his other fist, and began to chant. As the first drops of blood fell, I sensed a vibration in the deck beneath me, a thrumming as of a plucked bowstring. My inner eye saw a lion, or a jaguar perhaps, given the locale, waking from sleep and sensing prey. *Alecto* was waking, stirring to life in response to the offering. The Confederate captain's expression of distaste and disapproval remained unaltered.

The priest—or perhaps "officiant" is the better

word, since I could discern nothing in the least holy or Christian about the proceedings—brought his chant, which was not in any Spanish I have ever heard, to a close, and I thought that we had reached the climax of the ritual.

I could not have been more wrong. Acting as one, the four men who had been standing alongside the officiant left the quarterdeck. Descending upon the wretched huddle of pressed men, they seized the nearest of them, one man to each limb, and bore him back to where their master waited, knife in hand. Still without speaking or exchanging a signal of any kind, they stretched out their captive face upward upon the table and held him there, his struggling body forced by the table's convexity into a curve that elevated his chest and upper torso.

The officiant seized the victim's shirt in one hand and pulled it aside. With his other hand he drove the black knife into the victim's chest and yanked the blade sharply upward. He plunged his left hand forearm-deep into the gaping wound, then drew it out again and raised it overhead. Gripped fast in his bloodstained fingers was his victim's still-beating heart.

Everything had been done so quickly that the chosen sacrifice scarcely had time to scream. Now, however, a fearful outcry arose from the remaining captives, who saw in their comrade's fate the outline of their own. The officiant cast aside the dead man's heart, and his four henchmen seized the body once again by its four limbs and dragged it from the table.

Then, at a word from their master, they descended once again upon my fellows in misfortune.

Bound and guarded though the captives were, some of them at least were determined not to submit to their fate without a protest. The second victim singled out by the dark priest's acolytes proved to be one such. His struggles required the efforts of all four men to control him, and stirred the prisoners lying near him into a frenzy that drew the attention of their guards.

Another man, in civilian attire, lurked in the shadows. Now he stepped forward. I recognized that fellow from pictures; it was the same William Walker who so troubled Mr. Vanderbilt's soul. I wished then for my service revolver, to resolve the problem by the direct Army method.

The struggling man was brought before Walker, who appeared of mild, even amused, expression.

"You, at least, are destined for glory," Walker said, in English, and reached out his hand, placing it on the thrashing man's forehead.

At the moment of the touch, the man stiffened like one seized by rigors. His back bent until it seemed that his head should touch his heels, then straightened. And his flesh seemed to melt from his bones, and re-form into a different shape, until standing face-to-face I saw Mr. William Walker gazing into the eyes of an identical semblance of William Walker.

The four muscular men who held the victim's limbs gave a jerk at once backward, and the wretch who had been hauled up from the deck appeared again slumped between their arms. He seemed insensible—he did not stir, nor cry out, even as he was stretched face-up on that dread altar. The feather-clad officiant treated him even as he had the first victim, but my eyes were elsewhere. I was observing the two Walkers, more alike than twins, who stood in close and quiet conversation, the Confederate captain listening intensely to their discourse.

The four rough men had laid aside the new-made corpse, and turned again to the unfortunates on the deck.

I knew then that I would have no better opportunity for escape. I have no doubt that except for rapid action, I would eventually join the pile of dead. The War Department needed to know what I knew now.

My feigned unconsciousness had spared me further manhandling, and had kept my arms and legs unbound, and as the last of the potential sacrifices to be hauled aboard I had been set down the farthest from the killing table and the nearest to the ship's side.

After so long a time spent motionless, there was neither grace nor agility to my movements. I did not so much leap for the ship's rail as roll and scramble toward it on all fours; but I can truly say that what my progress lacked in dignity it made up for in speed. There was an outcry behind me—the sound of running footsteps pounding on the deck—and a second later I was tumbling over the rail and falling into the dark and welcoming waters of the lake.

Of the swim to shore, and of my journey through

the forest afterward, there is no need to write here at length. I owe my survival to the efforts of my guide Tomás, who—having chosen to disregard my expressed intention that he stay clear of trouble in San Anselmo—found me by the shore of the lake on the second day. I will put these journal entries into better form when we reach Managua; until then, I can only say that Mr. Walker's secret project is not a cannon foundry, nor even an ordinary ship of war. Every sailing vessel has a soul—even in the Artillery we know as much—but a ship's soul is nothing like whatever hell-born thing it is that Walker and his dark priest have called forth.

Alecto's indwelling spirit requires feeding—requires the sacrifice of human hearts and human blood—in order to make itself manifest. I tremble to think what kind of power and ability such a ferocious appetite has brought with it into the world.

I saw *Alecto* one time more.

From the shores of Rio San Juan, she moved like a ghost in the moonlight down the river, her masts and yards shining like silver. If the preparations were not complete at the moment I witnessed them, perhaps my escape forced their hands, and made her take to the open sea sooner than planned. My military training tells me that if one cannot defeat the enemy on the field, at the very least disrupting his plans is a worthy result.

One odd thing: I was looking down upon the ship's deck as she passed beneath my vantage point, and I beheld one whom I took to be Walker on the quarterdeck, dressed as he had been on that fatal night, and the Confederate captain beside him. Yet while that officer cast a shadow on the deck in the moonlight, Walker did not.

I report merely the fact as I observed it.

*The narrative of Lieutenant
John Nevis, USN, continued.*

IF THE CAPTURED REPORT TO THE FRENCH MINIS-
tre de Marine had been unsettling, Captain Bartlett's
account had a far more pronounced effect. I was ap-
palled by its revelations, and found myself hard-
pressed not to let the disquiet show in my features.
Miss Abrams plainly felt no such obligation; she had
the wide eyes and the pallor of one who has gazed
upon inward horrors. Captain Sharps, for his part,
showed no emotion at all, save for a certain satisfaction—almost, one might say, smugness. He looked,
in fact, as a man might who considers himself to
have been vindicated.

When the reading was done, the ambassador replaced the papers in his desk drawer and turned to
the naval attaché. "Lieutenant-Commander, please
provide our guests with everything they need. Captain Sharps, if you would be so kind as to provide
us with an itemized accounting—"

The captain at once turned his mild blue eyes on

me. "Johnny, tell the lieutenant everything. What stores and supplies. We are going hunting."

"Hunting, sir?"

"For a ghost."

We returned to the south of England in the ambassador's coach the next morning. Lieutenant-Commander Randall and I had fixed on the Azores for our resupply, with what I believed to be a reasonable assurance that all would prove as he suggested. The arrangements that we had made between us seemed to have met with the captain's approval, for when I raised the subject of ammunition he waved his hand and said, "I trust you, Johnny." It was the greatest word of praise I had yet heard pass his lips.

Miss Abrams, I believe, did not find the coach travel easy, for she appeared pale and remained silent during the entire journey.

Shortly after our arrival at the pier where we had landed the day before, I saw the longboat depart *Nicodemus* where she lay anchored in the stream. The boat fairly flew over the water; I expect that the prospect of bringing back our fair passenger lent strength to the sailors' limbs. Miss Abrams was handed down into the longboat, Captain Sharps took his place in the stern of the craft, and I cast off the painter and clambered down to my place in the thwarts. Again Ensign Bash was boat officer. His cheek was pale, though, and I could not avoid suspecting that something had gone amiss in our absence.

What had gone wrong, and how badly, I discovered soon after returning aboard. Lieutenant Dodge had taken command while Captain Sharps was ashore, and now he stepped forward, saluted, and said, "Sir, there has been an event during your absence."

The captain did not speak.

"Sir," Dodge said. "I fear there has been a desertion. Roger Wharton, able seaman, has not been seen since the first watch. A search of the vessel, so far as permitted, has not revealed his presence."

The captain tapped his foot, his only sign of interest, and turned to Lieutenant Cromwell, the engineering officer. "And is your space secure?"

"Yes, sir. I checked it at once. The seals were undisturbed, and so they remain."

Sharps turned to Miss Abrams. "Miss Abrams," he said. "Do you feel that this man has harmed the ship?"

She hesitated, and said, "Not yet."

"Very well. Muster the crew."

Drums beat out the command, and a short time later, it was so. The captain stood on the quarterdeck with Miss Abrams at his right hand, looking out over the sailors and petty officers assembled. I stood with Mr. Bash and Mr. Cromwell and the other commissioned officers in a separate rank by the fife rail. Perhaps it was lingering memories of Captain Bartlett's report concerning CSS *Alecto* that called up to my mind the events he had witnessed aboard that unhappy ship; or perhaps it was only the more recent memory of Lieutenant Dodge's wretched discomfiture under the captain's penetrating eye.

As soon as the echoes of drumbeats and tramping feet had died, the captain withdrew from an inner pocket of his uniform coat what appeared to be a small brass gong about the size of a hand mirror, set in a kind of bracket, or frame, of wood. This he handed to Miss Abrams—who received it in a manner more dutiful, I thought, than happy in her position—and turned his gaze again to the assembled crew.

"Gentlemen," he began, in a quiet but carrying voice. "We have come a long way, and sailed in a way that no man who ever saw the stars has sailed before. I have known most of you the better part of a year. Now Roger Wharton is missing. Did he talk to any of you about his plans? Speak!"

With this, he struck the brass gong a single time with his forefinger, as one might tap a melon in the marketplace to check it for ripeness, so that a single clear note rang out.

Again he said "Speak!" and again struck the gong.

A third time, and this time Jenkins—a man of the port watch whose hammock was slung next to Wharton's—cried out aloud: "Sir, he said he wouldn't be half a mile from the poxiest whores in all the Atlantic 'less he could have 'em, sir."

"Have you more to say?" the captain asked, mildly.

Jenkins's face was slick with moisture.

"Sir, he swum. Said he'd be back by light."

"Perhaps he is drowned," Captain Sharps said, in a musing voice. Then more loudly: "Mr. Dodge— you will take eleven men, neither more nor less. You will search the taverns, bawdy houses, and stews of this port until you find Roger Wharton, or until his bloated body washes ashore. If you lose a single man, or if you trade a single word with a civilian or sailor ashore, I assure you that you will wish you had not. I shall be in my cabin."

With that he turned on his heel and went below. The master at arms dismissed the men, while Lieutenant Dodge called the officers to him.

"Each of you," he said. "Pick the two most trustworthy men in your divisions. Send them to me." His face did not betray any great happiness.

I found Gunner Bellevue and Seaman Trask, and gave them into Lieutenant Dodge's care. They skipped out the boat boom and down the Jacob's ladder into the longboat, and cast off.

I remained on deck, looking over the rail at the city. The afternoon came on, then sunset, then twilight, then dusk. We hung lanterns in the rigging, as befits a friendly vessel in a foreign port. I could smell a churchy smell from aft, as though someone were burning incense.

As the sky blackened and the stars appeared, I became aware that Miss Abrams had joined me. She did not stand too close, but still close enough to speak in a low tone.

"John," she began. "Lieutenant Nevis. I fear that I have displeased you."

"Miss Abrams," I said. "That is not a matter for concern."

"Still . . . we have lost the comfortable discourse we previously had with one another."

This was no easy charge to answer, for there was indeed some truth in it. I found it difficult to speak at any length with Miss Abrams without images of her as she had appeared during our sea fight with the Confederate vessel arising to discomfit me and render me tongue-tied in her presence.

"It does not matter," I was finally able to say, "nor is there cause for you to please or displease me, for your health and safety is my duty, and my duty shall be done."

I thought perhaps she might speak further, but I heard only a quiet sound that might have been a sigh. After an uncomfortable moment she moved away and vanished in the darkness.

At length, there came a sound of oars. "Boat ahoy!" sang out the lookout.

"Hello!" cried the approaching craft. "Permission to come aboard?"

It was Lieutenant Dodge's voice. I was the only officer on deck so far as I was aware.

"Granted!" I cried back.

A moment later, sea painter and lizard line attached to the Samson post, the first sailors clambered aboard.

"Rig a block," said one, and soon they had a single whip attached to a main yard.

"Haul away."

And they brought up a limp man, a bowline round him under his arms, and laid him out on the deck.

Mr. Dodge stood beside me, watching.

"Wharton?" I asked.

"Indeed."

"Is he dead, or just dead drunk?"

"The latter, I'd guess."

At that moment, Captain Sharps himself materialized out of the night. He was once again wearing the eccentric uniform he had adopted for our sea fight.

"Make all preparations to raise anchor," he said. "We sail. At once."

Then he looked down at the still form on deck. "Bring that," he said, "to my cabin. Look lively now. Make a course for Biscay. Inform me of any ships or of the close approach of anything you do not understand."

Again, he turned on his heel, leaving Mr. Dodge and me to look upon one another like a pair of buffoons at the circus.

"You heard the captain," Mr. Dodge said after a moment. "See to it."

I summoned Trask and Hopkins, and relayed the order. They looked as dumbfounded as myself and Mr. Dodge, but bent obediently to the work. Then

Hopkins, who had taken Wharton by the shoulders, paused.

"Mr. Nevis, sir," he said. "I can't feel a heartbeat. I think he's dead."

"Are you a medical man, Hopkins?" said Mr. Dodge.

"No, sir," he said. "Just an ordinary seaman, sir."

"Captain Sharps is acting as medical officer for *Nicodemus*," Dodge said. "Wharton's heartbeat is his concern, not yours."

Hopkins fell silent, and he and Trask conveyed the limp form of their shipmate to the captain's cabin as directed. Some hours later Wharton emerged and joined his shipmates, and it was with some relief that I told myself Hopkins had been wrong after all.

The events of our last night in Portsmouth had been disquieting. Nevertheless, I might have been able to put them out of my mind, had it not been for the sequel which occurred a few nights later, when Gunner Bellevue approached me as I stood by the main shrouds on the starboard side. His face was a pale oval in the moonlight.

"Sir," he said.

"Good evening, chief," I said.

"A fair night," he said. He stood expectantly.

"What is it?" I asked, perhaps more sharply than I should have to one of the more experienced men.

"Sir," he repeated. "It's the crew. There's talk."

His words filled my heart with anxiety. There had not been an attempt at mutiny on board a Navy ship since the affair of USS *Somers* in 1842, and little good had come of that to anyone.

"What do they talk of?" I asked, fearing the answer.

What I heard, however, was not what I had expected. "It's Wharton, the lad who went ashore in Portsmouth. Some of the men don't like him."

I remained silent, allowing Bellevue time to continue his narration. *Nicodemus* cut on steadily through the water, with no sails set. What had seemed rare and remarkable only a few weeks before, by now had faded into the background of my concern. I had observed Wharton's altered demeanor with my own eyes; nor could I readily forget that his return had been the occasion of strained words between Miss Abrams and myself.

At length Bellevue continued: "He's—well, he hasn't spoken since he came back aboard. Not a word."

"Perhaps—"

"That isn't all of it, sir. The men are saying, some of them, that no one's seen him eat, either. Not since he came back aboard. He pulls on the lines beside them, but he doesn't look at them, and he doesn't talk, doesn't eat, and doesn't drink. Sir, some of the lads, they don't think it's natural."

"Do you think," I said—perhaps hastily, and certainly unguardedly to a seaman, even a petty officer like the gunner—"that anything at all we've seen since boarding *Nicodemus* has been *natural*?"

"Sir," the gunner repeated, "there's talk."

With that he faded into the darkness, returning, so I surmised, before the mast, and leaving me to my own uneasy thoughts.

Letter of Mark N. Chalmers, CSA, to Commander James D. Bulloch, CSN. Confederate wheel cipher, keyword JERICHO.

APRIL 15, 1862

SIR,

Pursuant to your orders I have maintained my position in the employ of the Federal Minister Plenipotentiary. Last night came three visitors, two in naval uniform and a woman. I was placed without the chambers to guard against interruption by the household staff.

The discussion centered on a letter written in French, which was not read aloud and thus I do not know its contents, and on the Nicaraguan intelligence report of which you are already aware. Of the three visitors, the younger man was a lieutenant who answered to the name "John Nevis"; and the female was referred to by both the two naval gentlemen and by the Minister himself as "Miss Abrams." The elder officer, who wore the rank of captain, did not state his name in my hearing. All three, I am given to understand, are attached to USS *Nicodemus*. They appear to have sealed orders of an unusual nature, which I will attempt to discern.

Other persons present at the meeting included a civilian—an Englishman or Scot from the Border region who gave his name as "Armstrong"—and the naval attaché.

The discussion after the reading of the letter was primarily between the young lieutenant and the attaché, on the subject of obtaining refits and supplies. Delivery for these stores was fixed on the 10th of May, but the place was not determined as I could overhear—either on one of the less-frequented Channel Islands or at a bay in the Azores. The supplies in question are to consist of twenty casks of fine powder, and twenty score of balls, the same size as those required for ten-inch Rodmans, but made of virgin brass. The lieutenant was very adamant on this subject: The brass must not have been used for any other purpose prior to the casting.

One may infer from the stringency of this requirement that the efficacy of either the ship or the weapons aboard her can be compromised by the introduction either of base metal, or of metal previously devoted to some other purpose. Very few places in England are capable of casting brass ammunition. I therefore recommend either a) sabotaging the brass by adulterating it in some way, or b) intercepting the delivery. Or, c) both.

Yours, very respectfully,
Mark N. Chalmers
Major, CSA

From: Henry P. Taliaferro
To: Commander James Bulloch, CSN, London
Confederate wheel cypher, keyword CATHAY

SIR,—

Pursuant to your orders, obtained entrance to Elkington and Co., Birmingham. Elkington has own copper refinery and took in hand Yankee contract for 400 cannon balls of virgin brass.

Order will require three casting days, with the foundry pouring day and night. Another week required previous to cleanse the crucibles of traces of non-virgin brass.

Non-virgin brass obtained, will introduce into crucible prior to casting. Awaiting further instruction.

From: Commander James Bulloch, CSN
To: Captain Fitzhugh Delahanty, CSN,
commanding CSS Alecto **Confederate wheel**
cypher, keyword MONTICELLO

APRIL 17TH, 1863

SIR:

The Navy of the United States appears to have gained information on the existence and nature of your raider, or to have independently devised a vessel of their own similar in capability and consequence to yours, by name USS *Nicodemus*.

The 14th instant brought to London said vessel's commander, a man called Sharps, and various of his crew, including a civilian female. Inquiries into Sharps's history indicate that he was not in the naval service prior to the war; further inquiry, that he was a scholar of some variety. I would not convict a man on his *curriculum vitae* alone, but the list of his intellectual accomplishments is highly suggestive.

Captain Sharps called for stores and ammunition, which suggests that both are in short supply aboard *Nicodemus*.

It is my information that they will be found on the high seas near the Azores to effect cargo transfer on 10 May.

I trust this information will prove useful to you.

Respectfully,
Jas. Bulloch
Commander, Confederate States Navy

*Text of a letter from Mr. Alastair Armstrong
of Melrose to the United States
Minister to England.*

APRIL 26TH, 1863

TO: MR. CHARLES FRANCIS ADAMS, LONDON

Sir:

Pursuant to your orders that I should determine "What's that man over in France up to?" I can report that His Imperial Majesty Napoleon III is not presently engaged in supplying the Rebels with the iron ships that they, through the negotiations of their agent Bulloch, have desired of him. Alas, I fear that my efforts in carrying out this tasking may have prevented me from giving adequate attention to a more important line of investigation.

To wit: Just as the presence of one esoteric ship implies the presence of another esoteric ship (as we recently have had proof), so our efforts to support one such ship imply that the American Confederates are making similar efforts. Thus, after our conference in London, I turned my attention to who else besides our own suppliers might have received orders for unusual ammunition. When the sum of all my detailed inquiries was "No One," I did not consider my heart to be set at ease. Instead I turned my attention to our regular supplier, to investigate whether or not he might be following the contract to the letter. This I determined, and was well satisfied that he had done, although the casting had by then already taken place.

I then made inquiries at the inns and the public houses of the town as to whether any strangers had been seen about, or any persons asking for information about the order for round shot cast from virgin brass. Though I heard of no one, two things did appear that troubled me.

The first was that a Confederate citizen calling himself Hank Smith (though I know from prior acquaintance with the fellow that the name is an alias merely) had last been seen not far from Birmingham, not long before the casting was to begin. The second thing, more worrisome, was the report of the theft of a set of Mass bells from a Romish church on the very day that the virgin brass was to be smelted.

My informant, a day laborer who liked his bitter by the pint, was quite unaware of the significance. "Blast me," he said, "everyone in the parish knew they weren't gold. Naught but brass, the lot of them, not worth a cracksman's time." I stood him another round, but learned nothing more.

What I have, then, is not proof, but suspicion, but suspicion strong enough that I wish to examine those cannonballs before they are sent to your Federal friends. I shall journey at once to Portsmouth, and hope to arrive before the cargo sets sail.

Respectfully,
Alastair Armstrong
Melrose

*Text of telegram sent from Portsmouth to London,
27 April 1863*

BARK OF INTEREST WITH CARGO OF IN-
TEREST DEPARTED PORTSMOUTH ON
MORNING TIDE STOP REGRET UNABLE IN-
TERCEPT STOP

*From the private log of Captain Fitzhugh
Delahanty, CSN, aboard CSS* Alecto

THIS DAY ARRIVED A LETTER FROM OUR ENGLISH
friend, in cypher, which I presented to Mr. Walker,
or rather to the ambulant simulacrum which the
president of Nicaragua saw fit to send with us on this
voyage. As is my custom, I opened the letter, and
rendered the jumble of letters within to common
English, and went to Mr. Walker—for so we were
told to address the simulacrum, as if it were the man
himself and not a shadow merely—in his cabin.

As is his wont, he asked me to hold the pages of
the letter before him, and at his command I turned
the leaves, and at his command I took up pencil to
write his reply. He did not touch the leaves of paper;
nor have I ever yet seen him take a pencil in hand for
any task.

" 'From William Walker, President of Nicaragua,
present in spirit aboard CSS *Alecto*,' " he began, " 'to

Commander James Bulloch, CSN, in London'—you know all the forms of address, Delahanty; you can make it proper later—'your news that the Federal Navy may have constructed a ship similar to our own is unwelcome, but not unappreciated. William Sharps I know by reputation. He is a man of considerable learning in esoteric metaphysics, though of bizarre belief: He was dismissed from one academy with instructions never to return; it comes as no surprise to see him involved in this project. The roles of the younger officer and of the woman are less clear to me, but I anticipate that they will be revealed in time.

" 'The word that you send concerning the proposed resupply of the Federal ship shall be of more immediate use. Without necessarily engaging Sharps directly—he is, as I said, a formidable savant—I believe that I can make of this occasion an opportunity to slip an observer of our own aboard his vessel. His pride in his own cleverness shall be his downfall.

" 'Yours, and so forth and so forth, William Walker.' "

Walker's simulacrum, its speech ended, once again fell silent—a sign that I was dismissed from its presence. I departed his cabin accordingly.

*The narrative of Lieutenant
John Nevis, USN, continued.*

ON THE NINTH DAY OF MAY WE SIGHTED THE
Azores on the starboard bow, and made landfall at
Corvo to refill our water tuns. *Nicodemus* lay off-
shore that night on a sea anchor, her head into the
wind. On the day following, the sailors had a Rope-
yarn Sunday, being released from regular shipboard
duties in order to do mending and make repairs to
their personal effects.

Once again I was struck by the care which had
gone into our vessel's peculiar construction and
equipment: even the jack-knives and sewing nee-
dles with which the crewmen labored were made of
metals other than iron. I heard some grumbling on
that score, since the bronze was softer than what it
had replaced, and delayed the work with its need
for frequent sharpening—but for every sailor who
cursed the issued kit, at least one other spoke cheer-
fully of appropriating it for a memento when the

voyage was done, so I deemed the mood of the crew
to be nothing dangerous.

For myself, I spent the time in darning the heavy
woolen socks I had worn in Thule and the northern
Atlantic. Miss Abrams, I thought, found the sight
amusing; she was smiling to herself as she watched
me ply the needle, so that at length I put aside the
work and addressed her directly for the first time
since leaving Southampton.

"I see that my labors provide you with some di-
version," I said.

"I'm impressed by your skill," she replied. "Perhaps things are different at sea, but on shore it's a
rare man who can so much as mend a loose button.
Unless he is a tailor, of course."

"A man at sea must often be his own tailor," I
said. "And if a thing must be done, one should strive
to do it well."

Her cheeks colored prettily then, and she said, as
if abashed, "You are a better person than I, John
Nevis."

"How so, Miss Abrams . . . Columbia?"

"I am but a clumsy seamstress, my knitting is
lumpily atrocious, and as for my darning—I fear that
if I were to turn my hand to your work, it would be all
knots and puckers, and not fit to wear any longer."

"Lack of skill is not a default of virtue," I said.
"Otherwise, we should all be wicked, since one
man's lifetime is not enough to comprehend the
mysteries of every trade."

"Yes," she said. "But I abandoned my sewing and mending with a glad good will as soon as Captain Sharps—plain *Mister* Sharps he was then—offered me the chance to come aboard *Nicodemus* and do something more important, he said, than knitting socks."

"It's not every woman who would have done so," I said. I thought of those who had paid others to serve for them in the Army, and added, "Nor every man, neither."

"You console me greatly," she said. "Would it distress you if I continued to watch and admire your work?"

"I would bask in the warmth of your regard, Miss Abrams, like a seal upon a sunlit rock."

And so, indeed, did we pass the remainder of the afternoon, until such time as a cry of "Sail ho!" from the lookout broke into the calm. The British colors at the approaching vessel's masthead, and the time and place of the sighting, told us that we had found rendezvous with our resupply vessel, the bark *Amphitrite*, out of Plymouth.

They approached within hailing range, whereupon Captain Sharps gave a most astounding performance in instructing them by speaking trumpet. They were to approach no farther, he informed them, but rather should lie to. We for our part would rig fenders and sailcloth over the side of *Nicodemus*, in order that we might tie up alongside *Amphitrite* there in the deep water, without our two vessels ever touching paint-to-paint and wood-to-wood.

Our own coopers were to cross over to the British ship, carrying barrel staves and hoops with them. We would remove our food and other supplies from the barrels in which they had journeyed thus far, and transfer everything into fresh barrels constructed on the spot, made with copper bands in place of iron hoops.

By now all of us aboard *Nicodemus* were used to the ban on cold iron and bright steel, but the British captain was clearly nonplussed. At length, however, the resupply commenced. *Nicodemus* extended her yards and rigged burtons and whips to load supplies as they were brought above deck and transferred from one cask to another, then lashed in slings and carried across, and so into our own holds.

The work went slowly, and officers of *Nicodemus* were required to stand on the Britisher's decks to ensure that no man of either crew spoke to any man of the other, not to inquire after news from home nor even to borrow tobacco. The seamen of both ships disliked and resented the prohibition, and the British officers, for their part, plainly found it risible as well as peculiar. We of *Nicodemus* liked it scarcely better, knowing as we did that Captain Sharps, in his usual humor, was unlikely to praise any of us for seeing it carried out.

Happily, I was spared the thankless task of keeping the men silent, being charged instead with overseeing the reception of stores aboard *Nicodemus*. Food had been the last item packed in *Amphitrite*, and so was the first item across. Then came sailcloth

and cordage; then paint, poured cask-to-cask prior
to transference, and pitch, the same. The British seamen watching the laborious and finicking process
bore expressions of frank amazement; the faces of
our men evinced only weary resignation.

Powder came next, and was stowed in the magazines. Then came the brass shot we had requested
with such particularity, and at that time the diffi-
culties began in earnest. The shot was loaded into
wooden racks, and the racks into nets, thence to be
swung aboard. But as the first net was lifted, *Nicodemus* moved sideways in the sea, away from *Amphitrite*, pulling her with us sideways through the
water.

The lines connecting the two vessels creaked
alarmingly, and the stay holding up the boom
parted. The net of cannonballs fell to *Amphitrite*'s
deck, splintering the boards with their impact—but
far worse was the action of the parted line, which
shot back toward *Nicodemus* as it ran through the
blocks. The bitter end flew like a cracked whip and
struck Seaman Trask, assigned to my number two
gun, a ferocious blow across both thighs.

Blood spurted and he fell. He cried out once.

"All hands, return aboard," Captain Sharps commanded, and the boatswains piped the call. Then
the captain looked on the deck where my man lay,
and said, "Take him to my cabin. I shall attend him
presently."

With that we cast off, and stood a cable length
from *Amphitrite*. I gave orders to do with Trask as

the captain had ordered. Meanwhile Captain Sharps and Miss Abrams rowed across to *Amphitrite* in the jollyboat, stayed aboard her for one turn of the glass, and returned.

At that time Captain Sharps went into his cabin. Shortly afterward, Seaman Trask emerged, his trousers bloody and face pale. From that moment on, Trask did not speak again. Nor, the story soon ran below decks, did he eat or drink.

*From the personal diary
of Miss Columbia Abrams.*

MAY 10TH, 1863

TONIGHT I SPOKE AGAIN WITH LIEUTENANT NEVIS.
I cannot converse much with him during the day-
time; there are too many eyes upon us, and I believe
he fears the appearance of taking undue advantage of
his position as my shipboard guard and mentor. On
the open deck at night, there are only a few people
near enough to eavesdrop, but enough of them remain
within sight and sound of us that we can claim—in
the name of propriety—that we are always observed.

"Do you remember," said I, "the conversation that
we had some weeks ago concerning the natures of
ships and their souls?"

"I don't believe I have forgotten any of the matters
upon which we have conversed."

"I am . . . honored by that," I said. "But it is *Nicodemus* that is my present concern."

In the darkness, I could not make out his expression, but his entire posture took on a sudden new alertness. "You have noticed something that touches on the welfare of the ship?"

"Of the *ship* . . . that is, in part, the question. When you say 'Nicodemus,' do you mean the thing of wood, paint, tar, and hemp on which we stand, and which conveys us upon the ocean main, or is it the fellowship and hierarchy and devotion to a joint enterprise of all the souls aboard her?"

He was silent for a while, so that I feared I had pushed too hard and too far with my questions; but at length he said, "Both of those things, I think, and more. There's no good way to separate them—they're all one."

"Ah," I said. I lowered my voice; I could not say for certain that Captain Sharps would not like what I said next, but instinct bade me to take care. "Is this some other thing that I do not perceive? That is, the thing I have come to understand about *Nicodemus*— they are *not* all one."

"I beg of you, explain further."

"I shall try. There is *Nicodemus* the ship, and that is one thing—but it is material only. And there is the crew of *Nicodemus*, which is another thing and *not* material, save in the individual bodies of its members. And last, there is 'Nicodemus' itself, which is neither one of these, nor made from these . . . which is, in fact, alien to both."

"What do you contend that it is, then?"

"I think"—here I paused and lowered my voice still further—"I think that this ship was constructed from the beginning to be a cage, and that the being which we call 'Nicodemus' is imprisoned here in the place of the natural soul possessed by other vessels."

The lieutenant's voice was as low as mine. "To what purpose?"

"Whence think you comes our speed and steady motion?" I asked him. "*Alecto* is a spirit fed on blood— the report we saw in London made that much completely clear. I do not know what bargains our captain made, or with whom, to gain control of our more kindly spirit; but gain it he did."

"What you say would account for a great deal," he said, after a few moments of silent thought. "But in the end, I cannot see that the discovery alters our situation overmuch."

"I should rather think that it alters things a great deal," I said.

He shook his head. "Captain Sharps is still in command, according to regulations, and our mission is a lawful and justified one, if the reports we have are true."

"Lawful, perhaps," I said. "But justified? I know in my heart that no good can come of enslaving a spirit to do our bidding. Not when the war we fight is meant to bring an end to slavery."

"Some people might rather say we're fighting to preserve the Union," the lieutenant said. "Mr. Vincent, for one."

"Barely five months ago," I said, with some impatience, "the president put his signature on a proclamation saying otherwise. That makes a difference."

He shook his head. "Even if it is as you say—and I will be the first to admit that I have almost no knowledge of such matters—I cannot see any way to alter the current state of affairs. Short of mutiny, that is, and I would not speak of such a course even in jest."

I had forgotten that to sailors, mutiny is close to the unforgivable sin. I wished that Mr. Nevis could bring himself to think about it, all the same, for I was not sure we deserved to be victorious if our ship was drawing its power from the very thing we had resolved to fight.

At the same time, I did not wish to think about the consequences should we fail. If even a portion of what we had heard of her was true, CSS *Alecto* was entirely meet for destruction, and *Nicodemus* was the only ship capable of the task.

The Narrative of Lieutenant
John Nevis, USN, continued.

CAPTAIN SHARPS HAD LONG BEEN CAREFUL, whenever *Nicodemus* came in sight of land or other vessels, to have sails aloft and to refrain from uncommon turns of speed, and from impossible maneuvers such as those with which we had earlier defeated the Confederate raider. For that reason a false stack had been erected amidships, and the fire within it tended to by Miss Abrams in such a way that it smoked a foul black reek, in order that we might appear to be making way under steam.

So it was also at this time, while we lay to alongside *Amphitrite*. Not long after the conclusion of our resupply, and the return of Captain Sharps and Miss Abrams, a cry from our masthead of "Sail ho!" revealed three ships of the line bearing the colors of the king of Portugal, making way under steam. A short time brought those three in line-ahead abreast of us on the weather gauge. Before much more time had passed, they came within hailing distance.

"Ahoy!" rang out the cry from the centermost and largest of the three ships.

"Hello!" responded *Nicodemus* in turn.

Then a man on the deck of the lead ship—presumably the captain, from the gold braid and lacing on his uniform—spoke in English through a speaking tube: "I am commanded by the King of Portugal to inspect your vessel. Lie to while I send aboard a party."

He did not wait on permission. The echoes of his hail had not died before a small boat began approaching *Amphitrite* from the third of the three Portugees.

"The captain won't like this," said Lieutenant Dodge, who had the deck since the time of the *Amphitrite*'s hail. He summoned one of the ship's boys with a nod. "You! Fetch Captain Sharps from his cabin at once!"

The lad complied, and soon the captain emerged from his cabin in response to the summons. He appeared, I thought, less than amused by the Portugee's reported words. Seizing *Nicodemus*'s speaking tube from Lieutenant Dodge with every evidence of impatience, he cried out, "You shall not inspect me! Be on your way and I shall be upon mine."

The Portuguese officer made reply. "Captain, I am commanded by the king himself. You will lie to."

"Your king does not command me," Sharps replied. Under his breath, a moment later, he said to me, "Fetch Miss Abrams topside at once."

I hastened astern to carry out his command.

Aboard the Portuguese flagship, at the same time, a whistle blew, and all three vessels ran out their guns. The lead ship blew her whistle and came hard starboard to pass ahead of us, broadside to our bow. As I was making my way down the companionway I could hear our own drummer beating to quarters, and before I was wholly down the ladder a rapid lurch threw me astern as *Nicodemus* leapt forward at great speed.

I hammered with my fist on Miss Abrams's cabin door. "Miss Abrams!" I called out. "Miss Abrams! The captain desires your presence topside at once!"

"Shall I dress?" came the cool response from within the cabin.

"As you please," I replied.

My errand accomplished, I then hurried off to my own station midships forward. Up on deck our own guns were being loaded and pointed. *Amphitrite*, meanwhile, upon the first appearance of the guineamen's guns, had hoisted full sail and put the wind on her quarter, and was away for the horizon to the north. She fell away rapidly astern, and when I glanced again in that direction, she was gone.

Turning my eyes back to *Nicodemus*, I saw that she was cutting through the water at her wonted speed—yet we were not pulling away from the foreigners, and a glance over the side told me why. The water beneath us was running like a millrace and we were making bare headway against it. By way of contrast, the water fifty yards to either side of us betrayed no such agitation. Save for a steady groundswell and a few wavelets, the ocean was still.

"The bastard suspects more than he knows," Sharps remarked to Mr. Dodge within my hearing.

"Let us pray to God that he does not know more than we suspect," Dodge replied.

"Do not let me hear that name again," Sharps said. To my mind the sentiment verged upon blasphemy, especially in our peculiar circumstances, but I had no time to think upon it further. The captain was calling out to me where I stood ready to direct the guns. "Lieutenant Nevis—on my command."

"Sir," I said. "Our country is not at war with Portugal."

"By this time tomorrow we shall be," he replied.

A lone gun boomed on the Portuguese flagship, firing across our bow.

"I give you my final warning, sir," the Portugee cried.

"And I give you my final answer, sir," Sharps called back. Then to me: "Commence fire!"

The firing commenced fast and hot. I was proud of my gunners to be laying such rapid fire, but concerned that their shots seemed to be having little effect on our opponents. Fairly, they did no damage to us, either, though I attributed that good fortune to the offices Miss Abrams performed within her bronze circle abaft the beam. I hesitated to glance toward her station, for fear of scandal.

Captain Sharps climbed into the mizzen shrouds as was his wont, and there directed our course. But however we maneuvered, and whatever speed he called for, the Portugees matched us, nor could we pass under their sterns to rake them, nor surge ahead. The headwind that we battled tore the smoke from our sides, so that I could see splashes to either side of the enemy, but not a break in their sides could we obtain.

A wild conjecture then presented itself to my imagination. Had I been aboard any other ship, and being as we were in the midst of battle, I would not have spared the time to consider it; but to serve on *Nicodemus* was a daily reminder that the wonders of the invisible world were with us still. I was pondering how to broach the subject to Captain Sharps when Gunner Bellevue approached me and saluted.

"Mr. Nevis," said he. "Sir, our magazines are low."

This came as no news to me; for I inspected the magazines daily, and knew that the resupply had been interrupted. The report might, however, provide me with the opportunity to test my new-formed theory.

"How much powder and shot?" I asked the gunner.

"Six hundred round shot, by my count, and powder sufficient to fire 'em."

"Very well. Cease your firing."

The guns fell silent. Scarcely a breath later, a harsh shout sounded from aft. "Mr. Nevis, if you please!"

I turned to Captain Sharps, and said, "Sir. An experiment. Observe."

I turned to gun twelve, the farthest aft on the port side. "Load," I said to the gun captain. "Lay your aim carefully, and place the ball midships on that Portuguese bastard, 'twixt wind and water." Cannon smoke hung heavily about the Portuguese decks.

"Aye," he replied, and the men sprang to. He pulled the lanyard, and the cannon spoke. Shortly came a splash, on the far side of the Portuguese vessel.

"What does this portend?" Captain Sharps asked. "I grow weary of your impertinence, sir."

"Captain," said I. "That ball passed entirely through our opponent, without leaving a hole." I paused. "I believe, sir, that we are firing upon phantasms."

The captain spoke then: "Port your helm. Hard."

The sun swung across the sky. The shadow of the mast chased across the deck. The Portuguese ships turned with us, their guns booming all the while, yet the shadows of their masts did not move.

"By—Sir, I believe that you have spoken well. Stop, cease all forward motion."

The waters calmed around us; the wind abated.

"Since you are so observant," Captain Sharps said

to me, "take the jolly boat and a crew, and row out.
Board them if you can."

This, with the guns roaring, and with splashes
from cannonballs rising to either side. All illusion,
if my conclusions were accurate; but if they proved
wrong . . . I saluted, and turned away.

Soon enough I and the boatswain's crew were
dashing over the waves; the faces of the men were
stoic. They had seen the demonstration I had given
to Captain Sharps, but maintaining one's skepti-
cism in the face of cannon fire is not easy.

We approached the nearest Portuguese ship, and
the boatswain threw a grapnel. It arched up above
the Portuguese rail and fell back down into the sea.
The line attached to it extended through the solid
wood of the ship's side. I ordered the jolly boat forward again, and we rowed through the Portugee's
side as if it had been a wall of cloud rather than oak.

A sensation of cold flowed through me as we
went. I shivered, and then we were on the far side. I
looked back, and found I could see *Nicodemus* perfectly. The Portuguese ship had vanished. In its
place, floating in the water, I saw a baulk of wood
perhaps three feet in length.

I directed the men to approach it. Once there, I
did not like to touch it with my hand, but feeling
that it should be seen by Captain Sharps, I caused
the men to bring it into the jolly boat with boathook
and oar, and to lay it down along the keel, under the
thwarts.

After that, we turned back, and soon were once more alongside *Nicodemus*. When I looked back, the ship that I had seemed to approach, and which we had fought with powder and ball for two turns of the glass, had vanished.

*The narrative of Lieutenant
John Nevis, USN, continued.*

CAPTAIN SHARPS CAME DOWN THE JACOB'S LAD-
der into the jolly boat to observe our prize. If he experienced the same revulsion that I had felt upon
beholding it, I could not mark it in his countenance.
Instead he reached out his hand, touched the wood,
and laughed.

"A rare trick he's played," he said, with one of his
wolfish smiles. "But it will lead to his downfall, I'll
warrant."

"Whose downfall, sir?" I presumed to ask, emboldened by seeing my earlier conjectures proved
true. "Do you speak of the captain of that ship we
had word of in London?"

"The man who captains her is not the adversary
whose wiles should most concern us," Sharps replied. "Say, rather, the man who feeds her appetites
and tends her altar, whomever he may be; and that
man's master, whose greater knowledge first caused
her to be built."

"William Walker," I said. The Union agent's report was not the first time I had heard rumors of dark powers associated with the name of the self-made president of Nicaragua, though his account had been the most explicit and the most trustworthy. "But not in person, surely."

"To men like Walker, physical distance constitutes no barrier." The captain smiled a little. "He no doubt believes that he has drawn the wool over our eyes completely." He pointed to first one, then the other of the two remaining Portuguese ships, both of them—to all appearances—still wreathed in smoke and firing their guns. "Johnny, lad, you'll find baulks like this one there, and there. Go and fetch them back."

With that, he climbed back up the Jacob's ladder, and was gone. The men in the jolly boat had heard the captain's order as well as I had, and set out to do his bidding accordingly, while I sat in the stern sheets and pondered the latest revelation. By the time we had retrieved the other two floating logs, the sun hung low in the west.

Captain Sharps was waiting on deck for us when we brought the jolly boat back to *Nicodemus*. "Bring that lumber to my cabin," he said, and soon enough it was done. The Portuguese ships had quite vanished.

Then Captain Sharps called for the ship's carpenter to bring his tools and come aft. That worthy disappeared into the captain's cabin and some hours later came out again, leaving his tools behind. He said nothing of what had happened in the cabin—only walked forward and asked the cook for an extra ration of rum. The cook, seeing his face, gave it to him without any questions.

A little before six bells of the second dogwatch, Captain Sharps appeared at his cabin door and beckoned to the executive officer.

"Mr. Dodge," he said, "fetch me two seamen and eighty fathoms of line."

This was speedily done. At Captain Sharps's direction, the seamen stretched out two lengths of line along the main deck of *Nicodemus* from stem to stern, one to either side of the masts, with a third length stretched between the mizzen and the sternpost. A paint line was laid beneath the stretched cordage to exactly mark the centerline of the ship. Then the seamen carried forth from the captain's cabin a sort of tripod, made of wood cunningly joined. This tripod they fixed to the deck precisely on the ship's centerline, aft on the quarterdeck but forward of the wheel.

Lastly, the men carried out from the cabin a curious statue. It was made of raw wood, hewn (as was the tripod) from the three timbers with which we had fought a seeming gun duel for most of the afternoon. The statue appeared to be a carving of a dwarf, or perhaps of a twisted and compressed frog, for it partook of both their natures, being squat and of a nearly hemispherical cross-section, hollowed out below so as to fit on the tripod and swing freely upon it.

The misshapen creature had its left arm clenched around its belly and its right arm outstretched, showing to the world a clenched fist with a clawed thumb tucked between the fore and middle talons.

Once the tripod was fixed in place and the statue balanced on it to turn freely, the captain addressed his officers: "Gentlemen, I desire that you steer so that the arm of "—he paused, and seemed to think better of speaking the creature's name—" so that this arm points ever forward and lies directly upon the centerline. In this wise I will, through fortune, find that Rebel raider whose existence necessitates ours.

"For the Union," he concluded, "and the honor of the Navy."

His speech done, he took his accustomed place in the mizzen shrouds and scanned the horizon. The officers, meanwhile, informed their steersmen of the situation and their orders, and so carried them out. A lantern was placed just abaft the mizzen, to illuminate the line, so that we could hold to the course by night as well as by day.

As soon as our preparations were done, we commenced sailing. An advantage of our odd method of propulsion was that we did not need to trim sail, or tack, to maintain our course. And so we proceeded, with nothing to mark the venture, for some three days.

Shortly after three bells of the morning watch on the third day, the man upon our lookout sang out that an object lay in the water ahead. On closer approach, the object appeared to be a section of decking, barely awash. We hove to, and put over a small boat.

The floating object had indeed been part of a ship, with a bit of hatch combing attached, as well as a portion of what could well have been a fife rail. From the fife rail, three green and mossy shapes trailed in the water, lashed to it by lengths of hempen small stuff.

"Poor buggers," Lieutenant Dodge said, taking off his hat. "Lashed themselves to it for safety."

"Bad work to bury them," Lieutenant Vincent said.

"Worse not to," the executive officer replied.

So with pieces of sailcloth we wrapped them, weighted them down with links of brazen chain (for we had not the round shot to spare), and committed them to the deep. What ship the wreckage had come from, we never determined.

Captain Sharps did not speak during this period, save to recite the Office for the Dead. When our sad duty was done, he strode again across the deck to his cabin, pausing by the statue on its tripod to say, "We grow closer," followed by, "More speed."

Once more trusting to the arm of the creature— dubbed "Froggie" by the crew, who held it in deep suspicion, not to say dislike—we sailed, and two more days passed. The helmsman's skill kept the swinging arm of the captain's wooden frog-creature fixed toward the bow.

We were southing, and nearing the Line. The sea

had an oily sheen to it, leaden under leaden skies that promised a blow. The groundswell was running out of the northeast, a light air backing and veering south to west. The air did not trouble us, nor the swells; our wake stretched out ever unchanging, straight as an arrow astern to the horizon. On any other cruise but this, *Nicodemus*'s wake might have struck me as the most unnatural thing I had ever seen, but the competition, of late, made it the least of marvels.

The noon sunline, two days before, had put us at sixteen degrees north. Since then we had steered south. Dead reckoning put us on the equator and the oppressive heat confirmed it.

Crossing the equator is customarily marked with celebration and rude ceremonial, initiating those aboard ship who have not heretofore sailed beyond the northern hemisphere. Thus do the young pollywogs aboard become shellbacks, and so may consider themselves thereafter to be salty sailormen. For this reason I fretted when the day passed without word coming down concerning the traditional festivities and rites of initiation. I feared that the crew might blame the omission on the presence aboard *Nicodemus* of Miss Columbia Abrams, for the spectacle of King Neptune's Court is not meant for a young woman's eyes and ears.

I did not need to think long upon the subject before the interior voice of common sense pointed out that it would be a simple matter for Miss Abrams to seclude herself in her cabin during King Neptune's visit, well away from any rude behavior that might go forward. The interior voice proved less forthcoming on the question of raising the issue with Captain Sharps, and I remained in debate with myself on the matter for the greater part of the morning. I had not yet reached a conclusion when, near five bells of the noon watch, a delegation of men led by Ezra Hopkins, one of the boatswain's mates, approached Mr. Dodge, and entreated to speak to him.

Delegations of men are seldom a good sign, nor was this. Hopkins saluted and said to the executive officer, "Sir, the quartermaster says that we approach the Line."

Lieutenant Dodge did not look surprised to hear this; I suspect that his interior ruminations during the morning had closely matched my own. With visible reluctance, he answered: "Indeed, that is true."

"Sir," said Hopkins. His own demeanor was nervous but resolute. "Some of us were wondering when the captain intends to stop to allow King Neptune aboard, sir."

"The captain has not vouchsafed such information to me," said Lieutenant Dodge.

The crew members looked at one another, and at Lieutenant Dodge, and—expectantly—at Hopkins. The last named appeared even more uneasy than before, but visibly drew his will together and persisted, saying, "There was a vote, sir. It'll be bad luck if we don't acknowledge the King, sir."

"Who voted?" demanded Lieutenant Dodge.

"Everyone, sir," said Hopkins.

Lieutenant Dodge frowned. "While we fight for the Union, this ship is neither a republic nor a democracy. Go back and tell *everyone* to thank God that these are no longer flogging days."

With that he turned away, nor did the men speak. After a moment of confusion they retired before the mast, leaving the executive officer standing silent and gazing across the deck, to all appearances lost in thought. At that point my own thoughts reached a conclusion, and I approached him.

"Sir, I could not help but overhear."

"It is our duty to show no concern," he said.

He continued to look out into the middle distance; following his line of sight, I saw that the object of his contemplation was the captain's wooden compass-idol, squatting on its tripod. I wondered if Mr. Dodge had his own suspicions concerning the idol's true nature, and whether, like me, he suspected that the captain misliked the idea of allowing King Neptune to set foot on deck while Froggie was watching.

At length Mr. Dodge seemed to reach a conclusion. He nodded to himself and said, "Would you convey my compliments to the captain, and inform him of what you could not help hearing?"

I went to the captain's cabin, knocked, and at his command entered. Captain Sharps sat at his writing table; its surface was covered with sheets of paper, some of them plans and drawings but most of them filled with writing in unfamiliar scripts and languages. He looked up from his work as I approached.

"Well, what is it?"

"Sir," I said, feeling as unhappy for my part as the luckless Hopkins. "The crew is growing restless; they desire to hold a crossing-the-Line ceremony."

The captain fixed me with a cold blue eye. "I will not be stayed from my purpose. We have no time to lose."

"No, sir," I said. "Nor would it be a good idea to seem to bow to their whims, lest they forget who commands. Still, Mr. Dodge and I thought that you should be informed."

"Thank you. Please pass the word to my officers that I am aware of the situation, and that I will deal with this problem."

"Sir," I said, and hastened to obey.

Shortly thereafter, Captain Sharps emerged on the quarterdeck. He spoke to the crew: "Turn to, you bastards."

The men, however, did not immediately return to their work. Instead Hopkins, who had spoken with Mr. Dodge earlier, now approached Captain Sharps and said, "Captain, sir, without King Neptune's goodwill, we're not going anywhere but New York."

"I will not bandy words," Captain Sharps replied. "Go to New York if you will, be hanged as mutineers as you will be, and afterward you'll still pull the lines and holystone the decks for me." Then he raised his voice to say, "If any man thinks he can turn this vessel about, let him do so."

Hopkins stalked aft to the wheel, took it in his hands, and strained to put it over. At length he did so—but not a fraction did the ship's wake deviate.

"Now that *that* is settled," said Sharps mildly, "return to your station."

"Sir, we have grievances," Hopkins persisted.

"Silence."

And from that day forward, Hopkins did not speak.

From the private log of Captain Fitzhugh Delahanty, CSN, aboard CSS Alecto

MAY 12TH, 1863

TODAY WALKER'S SIMULACRUM CAME TO MY CABIN with his Indian sacrificer beside him and said, "The spirit is hungry."

I did not trouble to hide my distaste. "You know what is needful. Feed it."

The Indian gave me a look of scorn in his turn. It was Walker who stated, "The captives in the hold will not be enough. Not if we keep on at this speed and take the ship farther each day from the place of its beginning."

"What do your metaphysics say that we should do?" I asked him.

"The next ship you take, take men also."

"And if we do not see a Yankee blockader?"

"Find a ship. Take it."

I felt myself moved to the most vociferous of objections. "Bad enough that we are forced to nourish

Alecto's motive spirit with the blood of peons and bandits and the scrapings of Managua's jails," I said. "That we should debase ourselves by using honest mariners in the same fashion is unthinkable."

Walker shrugged. All lives are the same to him, I think, and he cares for none of them. "Either make sacrifices from what you capture, or make sacrifice from the men of your crew. The spirit sees no difference. And when she grows hungry enough, she will take without waiting to be fed."

"She will be fed," I told him, and he turned, his Indian opening the door for him, and departed, which did not displease me, for I desired to be alone.

It is a hard thing that this voyage has forced upon me, but I know what has to be done. Already I see reproach in the eyes of the common sailors. They are uneducated, but they are not fools. They have seen the spirit's increasing appetite, and our diminishing store of captives with which to feed it. Surely they know already that if I do nothing, they will be the next.

Alecto may claim all the crew of our next prize, which will be a sorrowful thing but in the end perhaps the most convenient. If she takes but a portion of the survivors, leaving the rest for me to deal with as I see fit, then the only thing to do afterward will be to dispose of all the witnesses. It is already bad enough that Bulloch in London suspects that the Federals are aware of our existence; Walker insists that the greater world cannot be allowed to learn the true nature of this ship. Nor will I and my men escape hanging if the world should come to know.

I will not dwell on what I fear may happen once this voyage is done.

There can be no survivors.

One way or the other, *Alecto* may yet have us all.

Letter from William Fowler, Able Seaman, aboard USS Nicodemus, *to his sister Margaret Chapman of Marblehead, Massachusetts.*

MAY 15TH, 1863

MY DEAREST MARGARET,

Your last letter reached me as we lay at anchor in Portsmouth. I trust that Lily's disorders that you spoke of have been set aright long since. The food aboard this vessel is tolerable—the best, I think, since I shipped aboard USS *Connecticut*. Far better than that aboard the old *Powhatan*. We had no liberty in Portsmouth, which some took hard.

Of Captain Sharps I shall have much to say when next I see you. Many odd things have occurred, and are still occurring; this letter may yet grow in length before next we make port.

I know that you have some skill at gazing in ink or still water, and though you never speak of it, I believe that you keep a sisterly watch over me when I am far away. I cannot imagine what you must have made of the things you have lately seen. Indeed, I am not sure what to make of them myself. To recount them all would take up more paper than I presently have at my disposal, so a single anecdote must perforce suffice.

Last night we were struck by heavy weather. *Nicodemus* was most fearfully tossed about on the raging waters, so that I was in great fear lest we should founder, for we had come broadside to the seas, unable to make steerageway. I and my messmates were engaged in working the pumps, and in checking the seams, when the boatswain approached me and said, "Will, my boy, you're the best splicer aboard. Bring your knife and your spike and come with me."

We were at that moment rolling most dreadfully. I followed the boatswain through the gun deck and aft to the officers' companionway, where the captain himself met me, and fixed me with a cold blue gaze.

"Do you fear death, Will Fowler?" he said, which both surprised and alarmed me. Many stories are told of Captain Sharps in the ship's mess, and I have seen with my own eyes that some of them are true.

"Yes, sir," I replied. "The same as any man."

"The boatswain tells me that you can splice a line," he said.

"Indeed, sir," I replied. "It is my art."

"He will do," Captain Sharps said, and dismissed the boatswain with a glance.

Then he turned back to me, saying, "You shall never speak of what you will see," and taking a lantern in his hand he led me Diogenes-wise downward to the third deck, where a Marine stood aft of a door. At a word from Captain Sharps, the door was unlocked, and the captain led me forward. The door locked astern.

The lantern he carried was hardly necessary. The whole space, which ran nearly the length of the ship to the bulkhead aft of the sail locker, was filled with a cold blue light—more like to fox fire than to any kind of flame, but many times brighter—proceeding from an object in the center of the space, a kind of man-high latticework globe, the purpose of which I could not determine.

Great lengths of twenty-four thread ran forward through the space from sheaves aft, looped about through sheaves forward, and ran aft again. Two sets of lines crossed aft; two more sets ran fore and aft, making a net of sorts around the wooden globe. Each line had a sphere—what appeared to be an iron ball—rove onto it. If it was indeed iron, then those balls were the only iron aboard *Nicodemus*.

One of the sets of line, though, lay slack, the ball no longer suspended but resting upon the deck, being held steady by Mr. Cromwell, the ship's engineer. I could see that the line that had formerly held the sphere had chaffed, crowfooted, and jammed in a sheave.

The captain pointed to the line and said, "Splice it so it may run."

"Yes, sir," I said, thinking that was easy enough. I took out my knife—made of brass like everything else metal aboard *Nicodemus*, save for those spheres—and set about finding sound line on either side of the chaffed section. As I was about to cut out the junk yarn, Mr. Cromwell said, "Sailor, is that necessary?"

"Sir," said I. "It is my art. If you want the line uncut I can knot instead of splicing, but it won't run through the blocks."

"Let them run," said he, as though the words pained him to utter.

I then cut the line to remove the cowtail. Captain Sharps snatched up the cut portions and put them at once in a small bag that he carried, while the propulsion officer looked stricken.

I unlaid the line a good half-fathom in each part, and commenced laying the separate strands into a long splice. This was soon done, for the line was hard enough. Two more times did the officers remonstrate with me: once when I placed the line on deck to roll it under my foot (as is the practice, in order to tighten the splice), and a second time when I commenced to trim the ends protruding from the splice.

"Must you?" said Mr. Cromwell.

"It is his art," the captain said; then, to me, "Proceed."

Again, Captain Sharps gathered up every fiber of cut line, and secured them. When I was done, the broken line was now whole. The captain himself escorted me out and sent me on my way again, saying, "You shall not speak of this to anyone."

My messmates, when I returned among them, did

as you might expect, instantly asking me where I had been and what I had done there. Then I discovered that the captain had spoken true—for when I opened my mouth to answer, the tongue cleaved to the roof of my mouth, though I could speak freely on any other matter.

The prohibition, whatever it is, apparently does not extend to writing; he said "you shall not speak," and speech alone is denied me. I intend to mail this letter at our next port call, as scuttlebutt says that we will put in at St. Kitts for water; and I hope someday soon to see you well.

Your devoted brother,
Will

*The narrative of Lieutenant
John Nevis, USN, continued.*

AT SUNSET, NIGH A WEEK AFTER WE HAD CROSSED
the Line, the lookout spotted a boat, far too small to
have come this far off shore. It held five men, two
living and three dead. We brought them all aboard,
carefully, and laid them on the deck near the waist.
The dead we hastily buried in the manner of seafaring men, as we had the three others before them,
while the captain said the words. Their flesh was
corrupt; they stank.

The two living, or partly living, men we stripped,
and threw their clothing over the side, for it was
both ragged and rank. Then we washed them, and
dressed them in dungarees from the lucky bag.
Captain Sharps commanded that they be fed on
wine sweetened with honey, which he provided
from his private stores; and Miss Abrams bathed
their sores with cool fresh water, where the salt had
flayed the skin from their flesh, and where the sun
had burned them.

Both of the surviving men were weak from their privations, and near to death. We made up pallets for them on deck, for the air was cooler there; also, despite being bathed they were fetid. Night fell. Miss Abrams sat with them, a hurricane lamp by her side, with a sailor assigned to carry out any tasks she might command. At three bells of the midwatch one of the men awoke and, raising his head, asked the name of our ship and where we called our home. He was well satisfied with the answer and gave this narration, which Miss Abrams wrote down in her journal as he spoke, and which she later read aloud to Captain Sharps and the other officers, including myself:

My name is Samuel LaFarge, able seaman aboard *Lucy Wainwright*, merchantman of Boston, Captain Richards commanding. We were under way with a cargo of crockery from Liverpool to Recife. On last Monday morning, just at daybreak, we were making way under topsails with a fresh quartering breeze, when the man at our masthead sang out, "Sail Ho!"

The vessel he had sighted was a three-master, hull down to lee. I thought no more about it, for she would have to beat a long way up wind to touch us, but beat upwind she did.

I had been set to rubbing down spun yarn, and took my place by the port cathead to do my work, where I could from time to time look out to lee. The other vessel was coming up under bare sticks, from which I supposed her to be a steamship; but this was far out to sea for any steamer, nor did I ever see smoke.

Ere two bells had passed, I could see plainly that the steamship—for such I still thought that she must be—was flying the Rebel battle ensign, and I thought, Samuel, my lad, now you're for it, I don't like the looks of this.

The *Lucy*'s mate appeared to be of the same mind, for he ordered full sail. Captain Richards liked the Rebel's appearance even less, for he had our guns run out: a pair of six-pounders on the quarterdeck, and a pair of swivels forward. So we continued, and I stayed at my work, for I was neither on the gun crews nor aloft.

The stranger, meanwhile, was coming up to us with great speed. Despite the wind, she was racing toward us like a dolphin, leaping through the waves. A queer gleaming came from her, as if she were sculpted of ice. She ran down our port side, then up our starboard, like a dog circling a rain barrel, then fired a single shot across our bows.

I thought I heard the captain say, "Not much doubt of *her* intentions," and he promptly ordered that the *Lucy*'s colors be struck, for we were heavily out-gunned, nor could we outrun such a rapid pursuit.

The Rebel ship took station ahead of the *Lucy*, and her master came on deck with a speaking trumpet. He ordered us to back our mainsails and heave to, which we did. Shortly afterward, he commanded that all aboard the *Lucy* should come on deck and kneel there, facing to port.

This too we did, for the Rebel's guns were pointed to rake us through. At length came a plashing of oars and the sounds of boots on the deck behind us, and we heard a voice shouting the command, "Eyes down, don't move."

Then we heard more boots, and a different voice saying, "Take this one, and this one . . ." as the speaker proceeded down the length of the deck. The man to the right of me, Davidson the ship's cooper, was chosen in this wise. He stood and was taken away.

Finally, although it had undoubtedly been just a few minutes' work, the boots stopped, and the oars sounded again, this time moving away. As I was looking around me in amazement, without warning there came a thunderous explosion. The deck rose beneath me, and I next came to my senses in the water. We supposed later that the Rebels had put a match to our small magazine.

As I struggled in the water, by and by came Mr. Arbiter, the third mate, in the ship's boat, with William, a foretopman, at the oars. By means of a boathook they plucked me from the water. Two more men we found, and took into the boat as well.

William died on the third day, and Mr. Arbiter and Joshua Daley, from Acton in Massachusetts, on the day after. Since then we have been floating, until we saw your sail.

* * *

Samuel LaFarge died just after sunup, for he was
very weak. His companion died the next day at
noon, never having regained consciousness, nor did
we ever learn his name.

From the private diary of Miss Columbia Abrams.

MAY 22ND, 1863

THE SUFFERINGS OF SAMUEL LAFARGE, AND THE statement he gave concerning the *Lucy*'s destruction, have disturbed me greatly. I do not want to think about why those aboard the Rebel ship—which is surely that same vessel *Alecto* of which we received word in London—might have impressed those members of the *Lucy*'s crew into their service; but I cannot stop myself from pondering upon that very question. The report from the Union agent in Nicaragua described a ship brought to unnatural life by the most dreadful of sacrifices. What if *Alecto* needs even more bloodshed in order to continue her operations?

"A hungry b—h." That's what the Union agent said they called her in Nicaragua. I wonder if she still feeds.

And did the prisoners taken off of the *Lucy* go to

sate that bottomless appetite, or were they merely taken in order to work the ropes, as the British did our sailors in 1812?

This is not something of which I can converse with Lieutenant Nevis. When it comes to pagan cosmologies and the darker metaphysics, he is (however amusing he might find the idea) still an innocent. Moreover, while we are once again speaking to one another, we have yet to regain that ease of social intercourse which we experienced prior to *Nicodemus*'s first sea-fight.

I would not like to discuss the matter with Captain Sharps, either. He knows, I am beginning to suspect, entirely too much about the darker metaphysics himself for me to feel comfortable broaching to him my suspicions concerning *Alecto*.

That leaves me with only one possible confidant: *Nicodemus* herself. I still do not know the precise nature of our vessel's indwelling spirit, but it does not require exact knowledge to guess that *Alecto*'s soul, if soul the Rebel has, is something of quite another kind.

Later—

I have spoken with *Nicodemus*. It was some hours ago; my hand has only now ceased shaking enough for me to write.

Conversation with *Nicodemus* is not entirely a matter of words. I speak aloud when I am alone with the heart of the ship, because that is how I can best master and organize my thoughts. The answers I receive are inarticulate—unknown emotions, unfamiliar knowledge, unbidden images, all entering my mind from other than the five senses. The experience can sometimes be exhilarating and sometimes refreshing; today it was neither.

I waited until after the evening rituals and chants to ask my question. I made sure to think very hard about the French ship's sighting of a mysterious vessel without steam or sails, and about Captain Bartlett's report from Nicaragua, as I said, "Nicodemus—do you know anything about *Alecto*?"

Uncertainty came first. Then I saw again the dehydrated and ulcer-ridden bodies of Samuel LaFarge and his compatriots, as they had looked when our crew brought them aboard; and after that, an image I had not seen with my own eyes, of three drowned men lashed to the wreckage of a ship's rail. Pale and bloated and fish-eaten—I had never seen them in that state myself. They had already been wrapped up in sailcloth for burial at sea before I came on deck.

"Yes," I said. "*Alecto* did that. Can you"—I had to grope for words to explain what I wanted; it is not an easy thing, to speak of distance and travel to someone, or something, that is essentially incorporeal—"are you able to look farther away from—from yourself, and see where *Alecto* is, what she does now? In the same way that the captain's eidolon looks for her?"

An image of the rough wooden image the sailors called Froggie came to me, accompanied by a wave of scorn so strong that I laughed despite myself.

"You don't like our ugly friend? Neither do I, if you want to know the truth. But he'll do for pointing out the way, since the captain didn't think to ask you the same question."

Another wave of scorn. As I have remarked in these pages before, I do not believe that *Nicodemus*'s indwelling spirit cares for our captain much at all.

"Yes, yes . . . but would you do it for me—*could* you, if I asked?"

Willingness, coupled with uncertainty.

"If you could try—"

Of a sudden, I had the same bird's-eye view of the deck as I had experienced during my very first conversation with *Nicodemus*, only this time obscured by the veil of night. I could see John Nevis was on watch—the observer from on high swooped down for a moment in a dizzying spiral and circled him where he stood gazing out over the moonlit ocean, before darting forward and away, arrowing toward the horizon. Sea and sky blurred together at exhilarating speed; the observer—which was, I understood, as much *Nicodemus* as the wooden vessel in which my body still stood—moved at such a great rate that I could not tell how much distance was being covered in our progress.

Then I saw ahead of us a vessel with mast and yards that shone like silver. *Nicodemus* slowed and once more spiraled downward until the vessel's deck came into view.

Yet at the same time it was not a ship: It was a darkness, a jagged outline of red and gold that broke apart and reformed again and again, while the air pulsed against me, and heat seared me, and my tongue parched. It did not so much sail upon the water as float above it, and did not so much move forward as vanish at one place and reform at another slightly more advanced.

It came to me that the pulsing in the air was of the same speed and quality as a heartbeat, and that its rate was increasing. Faster and faster came the pulses, wider spread the obscurity, until there came a supreme paroxysm and the lines of red and gold flared, too bright to look upon. I closed my eyes; the heat seared my lungs, and . . . I must have swooned. For I awoke, curled into a ball like a small child, alone and naked on the cold lower deck of *Nicodemus,* the pale-glowing wooden sphere before me, and all contact with its spirit withdrawn from my mind.

I dressed, and returned to my cabin.

Before I departed on this journey, my Aunt Sophronia pressed upon me a bottle of French brandy, "For the sea air, my dear." It stands now before me. Perhaps a teaspoonful will settle my nerves.

*The Narrative of Lieutenant
John Nevis, USN, continued.*

TWO WEEKS AFTER PLUCKING THE REMNANTS OF
Lucy Wainwright's crew from the sea, and subsequently burying them in it, we were sailing near
due south, as close as anyone could make without a
compass on board, our speed twenty knots good
over ground.

The air was cool, for mid-winter approached in
Southern latitudes. The wind was out of the nor-
nor-west, having backed from the south during the
first watch. The dawn was red, with mare's tails
and fishes' scales away to the west; during the day
the clouds gathered and lowered, the glass dropped,
and the seas became confused.

Of a sudden the man on the foretop cried, "Sail
ho, dead ahead, three leagues off!"

At the cry, Captain Sharps emerged from his
cabin and went at once to the quarterdeck where
Froggie still crouched on his tripod, outstretched
arm and clenched fist pointing the way for the man

at the wheel. The captain placed the flat of his hand atop Froggie's misshapen head and stood for a moment with his eyes closed as if in thought. Then he said, calmly, "Beat to quarters."

In an instant it was done. After the weeks of inaction a thrill ran through the ship. All could feel it. At the same moment, the first lash of rain fell, sweet water amidst the salt spray. I glanced at the glass. It had fallen since the last bell.

Miss Abrams then came up on deck, her Attic robe fluttering around her bare ankles in the rising wind. Her hair was unbound already—or perhaps she had not yet put it up when the summons came. The men scarcely paid her heed; so readily, it seems, does the strange become commonplace. By this time Captain Sharps had rejoined us on the quarterdeck, dressed now in his outlandish fighting rig.

"Sir," I felt compelled to say. "Do you desire me to load? We have at present shot for six full broadsides to either side."

"Load, Mr. Nevis."

"Sir," I said, and hastened to do his bidding.

Nicodemus was at this time proceeding at tremendous speed, casting up white spray above the catheads as she cleft the water. Soon enough, those of us on deck were able to see what the man on the lookout had earlier reported, and what the captain—through Froggie's agency—had somehow perceived. Ahead stood a Spanish man-of-war, her courses reefed up for battle and her hull surrounded by powder smoke, while round about her prowled a low black-hulled vessel under bare yards, yards that shone with the lustre of silver. The horizon beyond the two ships was lost in flying scud, the clouds lowering to fog in the distance.

I called to mind the Frenchman's account that I had read in London, of the dark silent vessel companioned by sharks, and could not suppress a shudder. Spain was no ally of the Rebels, but no enemy either; it would seem that the "hungry bitch" had grown hungrier still, and less discriminating.

Others of the crew, it seemed, had a more recent encounter in mind. Gunner Bellevue spoke to me quietly as we stood by the guns. "Are we sure we aren't fighting a ghost, same as we did with those Portugees?"

"The captain is sure," I replied.

"Cap'n was sure the last time, too."

The ship pitched as she cut through the swells. I let the gunner's comment go unanswered. Little good would come of casting doubt upon the captain's judgment; and besides, experiment would soon settle the question.

"Load both sides," I said, "and stand by to fire."

"Aye aye, sir," Bellevue said with a salute, and turned to exhort the gun crews.

The rain commenced in earnest then, stinging with its force. Miss Abrams took up her battle station in the brass circle, in full exposure to the elements. Her robe was soon wet through and plastered to her body, while her hair hung in lank strands down her back. Her expression was unspeakably grim. I thought of what she had said to me about the nature of *Alecto*'s spirit, and of her surmises about our own ship's captive soul.

Now the black-hulled vessel broke off. The Rebel battle ensign stood out from her mizzen as she abandoned her prey and came about, and the seas broke across her deck with green water as she turned.

"They'll have as much trouble with their powder as we do," I said to Gunner Bellevue. "And that's a mercy."

The Spaniard lost no time in breaking out full sail and turning downwind to run for the horizon. Nor could I blame him: in a sea fight between two such ships as *Alecto* and our own *Nicodemus*, a common vessel would be as a sparrow caught between two eagles. Captain Sharps, meanwhile, took his place in the rigging, and cried out to the crew: "Now, men, let us show these Rebel dogs what we are made of. There sails *Alecto*, the ship we have crossed so many leagues to fight. The day shall be ours!"

Lieutenant Dodge led the men in three rousing cheers. The wind freshened, carrying the sound like a challenge across the water in the direction of the Rebel sloop. Captain Sharps beckoned to me.

"Johnny, my lad," he said. "When that Rebel pirate closes a bit, I shall come hard left to give your starboard broadside a shot. Take it."

"Aye aye," I said, and gave the word to the gunner and the gun captains: "Stand by and look sharp. We shall test ourselves today. I have every confidence in your skill and your spirit."

By now the wind was taking the tops off the whitecaps and spreading them as foam and spray down the sides of the waves. The rain came slashing down, fresh water from the roiling clouds above mixed with the ocean's windborne salt. My boat cloak was soaked through, but thanks to the good wool of its construction, protected me still.

I thought of Miss Abrams, already bare of arm and shoulder in her antique robe, and in the heat of battle soon likely to be barer still. I would have gone to place my cloak around her shoulders, but that I was unwilling to chance impeding her work on our behalf. Only the fact that rain and spray alike were blood-warm made the thought of her situation bearable.

I looked again across the turbulent expanse of water that separated us from our long-sought quarry, now turning to the attack. Trails of smoke or mist flowed from *Alecto*'s mastheads and yards, as if she were all on fire but not consumed. Waves crashed on her bow as she came on, and the wind keened in her rigging.

On, still on she kept coming. A single cannon fired from her bow, the smoke of its discharge rapidly blown astern. I did not see where the ball fell, for at that moment Captain Sharps ordered, "Hard a-weather! Stop her!" We heeled over as our head fell away to the left, and I was hard put to keep my feet as we suddenly slowed.

The waves struck us now on our port side, spray shooting above the rails and rising like a waterspout toward the heavens. The impact was severe, but we stood as if *Nicodemus* were a rock in the midst of the ocean, not rolling nor pitching in the slightest. When I looked up over to starboard, there was *Alecto* showing her bow aspect, the white waves curling away to either side of her as she came up.

"She has a bone in her teeth," observed Gunner Bellevue. "I didn't think there was a ship afloat that could match *Nicodemus* for speed, but this one comes close."

"She's full-up with wickedness," I said. "But lay your guns well, and we'll rake her."

For I knew that so long as *Alecto* came on without turning, we were in the best position ever a ship was in to take another vessel under fire: We could bring the whole weight of our broadside to bear while she had but a single chaser to return fire. More, each of our cannonballs would traverse the entire length of her deck, doing damage the whole way.

"Steady, lads, steady," said I; then, when the range had decreased, "Fire!"

Fire we did, and with admirable alacrity the gunners sprang to their tasks of reloading. As they did so, I counted off "one," and knew that I now had but a scant handful of broadsides available to me.

However terrible the damage we might have done *Alecto*, she did not waver in her course. As she came up, I could see black shapes that a casual observer might have taken for dolphins, playing at her bow.

As soon as ever our guns were loaded, with *Alecto* a pistol-shot away, I again cried, "Fire!" but while our balls were in flight *Alecto* came hard left, and what had been her bow aspect became her starboard beam.

I saw our shot fall harmlessly into the sea astern of her as she made to cross astern of us, close aboard. Now we would feel the weight of her shot against our unprotected counter. I glanced aft, and saw Colombia, hands aloft, standing in her accustomed place and in her accustomed state of nature. Perhaps it was the fierce expression on her face that made me pause.

My gun crews were again reloading. Low cloud and fog surrounded us, even as the wind made the rigging thrum. The horizon was utterly gone; all that was visible was perhaps a mile of ocean, perhaps less, an amphitheater with misty walls. I thought then that this must be how the ring appeared to a prizefighter. Rain stung my cheeks. With a sudden start, we began moving, and as we moved, we rolled, and came left, placing *Alecto* under our portside guns.

"Shift your side!" I cried; then, "Fire!"

I could see the brass shot as it flew, to take *Alecto*

on her starboard bow. At that same moment she pulled her broadside, and our sides erupted in splinters and spray. This time, unlike our previous gun battle with a Confederate ship, Miss Abrams's efforts did not see most of the cannon fire deflected away.

The splinters of wood thrown up by the impact of cannon shot make terrible wounds, nor was this an exception. Men fell groaning, while their messmates hastened to staunch the bleeding of their wounds and pull clear of their stations those too gravely hurt to work the guns.

No one stood on *Alecto*'s deck. Forward I could see the rough pyramidal table described in the reports that we had seen in London. All the fire was coming from the enclosed gun deck. I could see the muzzles pointed through the gunports, nine of them. I made them to be twenty-four-pounders.

If we cannot fight and win with a dozen ten-inch Rodmans against a common eighteen-gun sloop, thought I, then God has deserted us and we do not deserve victory. I counted again: three broadsides remained to us, and one of them was locked into our starboard guns.

"Load!" I ordered.

Mr. Dodge appeared at my elbow. "Captain wants one of their cannonballs," he said. "Got one?"

I looked about the deck, where I espied broken timbers, but no cannonballs. "Perhaps buried in the side?"

"Maybe." He continued forward.

We turned toward *Alecto*, and the boatswain's call sounded *Muster Boarders*.

"The man's mad," Gunner Bellevue said by my elbow. "Magnificent, but mad."

I knew he spoke of the captain, but held my peace. He'd named no names, and in any case I could not bring myself to disagree. To call for boarders, under such circumstances, was either a species of madness or a sign that the captain, by virtue of his learning in arcane matters, knew more about the nature of *Alecto*'s operation and defenses than he had vouchsafed to the rest of us. Only experience, in the end, would show which was the case.

I felt for my sword, then recalled that I had left it behind at Thule. A revolver and a rapier, or a good heavy axe—anything besides bare hands—would have given me more confidence; but all such close-in weapons, being made of steel or forged iron, had come under the interdict.

"Swab rods and handspikes," I said, as the boarding party began forming up midships. Sailors all; our small contingent of Marines would be needed in reserve, to repel boarders from *Alecto* and safeguard *Nicodemus*'s most secret inner workings. "And the bronze knives you have for shipboard use. Take heart; I imagine *Alecto*'s crew labor under the same constraints as we do."

"I don't have that much imagination," Bellevue replied.

At that moment *Alecto* turned away, and began to

run for the mist banks. We followed. Faster we went, and faster, the spray breaking upon us, the wind howling, the rain pouring so that we could hardly see our hands before our faces, and still *Alecto* ran, and still we followed.

*The narrative of Lieutenant
John Nevis, USN, continued.*

THE BOATSWAIN'S PIPE SOUNDED *OFFICER CALL*,
and I headed aft to the quarterdeck. Captain Sharps
was there, his hair plastered to his skull as he stood
bareheaded in the deluge.

"Gentlemen," he said, and held out his hand. In it
lay a shard of black, glassy material.

"Do you recognize this?" he asked in a conversa-
tional tone.

"It's a piece of rock," Ensign Bash said.

"Not just any rock," Captain Sharps said. "Obsidian. It's what *Alecto* is firing at us. Stone forged in
volcanic fires . . . I imagine their resupply problems
are greater even than ours. They too must be low on
ammunition, having fought their way by now across
two seas."

In the fog ahead of us, *Alecto* was little more than
a distant shape in the surrounding grey. Above the
storm clouds the sky was darkening. Night would
be coming soon.

"A stern chase is a long chase," Lieutenant Dodge said. "We'll lose her in the dark."

"I think not," Captain Sharps replied. He gave Froggie an affectionate pat on its wooden head. "Now I must study on matters as they stand. Miss Abrams, you may rest awhile; I do not anticipate needing your offices before dawn."

He departed in the direction of his cabin. Columbia followed, not bothering to replace the sodden robe that now lay in a puddle on the deck. As she passed by me, I placed my boat cloak over her shoulders. She cast a grateful glance in my direction, and continued on.

"Boarders forward," Lieutenant Dodge said to the men. "Stand by below decks, and be prepared for tricks. Double ration of grog to all hands. Pass the word, 'Well done, they're running.' "

Then he drew me aside. "I don't trust the Rebels a bit," he said. "Those bastards may have more tricks than the captain suspects. They gave us that wood"—Here he nodded at the heathen idol mounted on its tripod, its arm pointing forward once more—"and for aught I know they did it just to make happen what did happen. Now they're running, true enough; but that means they're leading. And we're following."

"What would you have me do, sir?"

"Nothing," said he. "Only this: Keep your eyes open and your ears sharp. Now I'll see how badly we're hurt, and look to repairs. It'll be a long night."

"Long night, aye," I answered, and turned to my own duties. The guns to either side were loaded. I ordered tampions put in and the touchholes plugged to save the powder and shot from the spray and the ever-falling rain.

Our recent engagement had left more men hurt or killed than we had suffered in all the cruise to date. Eight bodies lay under sailcloth on the gun deck. After nightfall the captain visited them alone, remained there with them alone, and returned to his cabin alone.

The eight men joined their messmates forward, but did not speak nor eat.

Night had fallen, moonless and starless. The ship hogged and sagged as we crashed through the swells whilst the rain fell in torrents, lashed by a howling wind. On deck only the steersman stood, the officer of the deck beside him. One lookout remained in the masthead forward. All others were below decks.

The pitching was so severe that no man could remain in the forecastle, but gathered midships on the spar deck, clustered in oilskins around a glimmering lantern. Pale, a ghostly crew—but living, holding themselves still aloof from the new-made walking dead, who stood a little apart with eyes gazing blankly forward.

The men were too exhausted to do more, nor could they sleep with the ship's motion. By turns they went to the pumps, for we were shipping solid water over the bow, which ran back to the hatches in the waist; water entered around them despite the battens and canvas. With every turn of the glass, four men went to the pumps to work the handles up and down, but we could not tell to what effect. Water came in, water went out.

I saw Lieutenant Dodge approach the boatswain and point to the dead men. "Make those your boarding party for tomorrow," said Dodge. "It'll be no greater loss if any of them come to harm."

The boatswain looked at the dead men where they stood in the shadows. "Just going near them makes my blood cold," he said. "Wharton and Trask were bad enough, and Hopkins struck mute, but so many all in a group—"

"Nevertheless," said Lieutenant Dodge, "it is your duty."

"Duty," said the boatswain. His voice was a low growl, so that I had to strain to hear. "I do not fear the devil, sir—but I do fear his works."

I saw Dodge grow tense; as well he should, for the boatswain's words tended in no good direction. "Do as I say."

"Do you hear what I'm saying, sir?"

"I hear you, Boatswain. Do not force me to take notice." With that Mr. Dodge turned away.

The boatswain took boathooks, brass heads on ash poles, belaying pins, and fids, and gave them to the dead. Whether or not they understood him, I could not tell, for they did not speak, but they did take up the makeshift weapons before returning to stand motionless in the shadows.

The boatswain was not the only man aboard to harbor such thoughts, though he was the only one bold enough to come near raising them to an officer. A little while later, I overheard the carpenter and his mate speaking to one another.

"I hope that we don't open a seam, what with this pounding," said the carpenter.

His mate nodded forward to the boarding party. "If we do, better to be with Davy Jones than like that. Do you think they suffer as we do?"

"I don't know," the carpenter said.

"Nor I . . . what time is dawn?"

"Two hours, I make it," said the carpenter. "Stand fast; dawn always brings hope."

The carpenter's mate shook his head. "For us, maybe. Not for them."

"There'll be action in the morning, sure enough," agreed the carpenter. "Do you suppose he'll try to board the Rebel then?"

No doubt, as before, as to who was meant.

"He's mad," said the carpenter's mate.

The carpenter shook his head. "He's damned."

"Then maybe so are we all."

Nicodemus heeled hard to starboard as a fresh gale took her on the port side. She came back slowly.

"Would to God that tonight were over," said Seaman Dow, another crewmember among those gathered around the pale light of the lantern.

Ensign Bash, who had just come down from the main deck, looked at him sharply. "Do not speak that name. Captain's orders."

I suppressed my feelings of disquiet at hearing this. An outside observer might have thought that Captain Sharps merely strove to curtail his sailors' habit of casual blasphemy (as another man of reforming character might be a teetotaler or an advocate of physical gymnastics—I have served under both in my day), but I suspected that reverence for the Deity played little part in the Captain's orders.

From the expression on Seaman Dow's face, the man agreed with my estimate. "Do you hold that correct, sir?" he asked Ensign Bash.

The ensign's cheeks reddened. "By God, I do not."

I feared then for a moment that I would have to intervene before the talk grew more reckless still, but they let it drop.

And thus the watches of the night passed. In the first watch a strake came free forward on the starboard side, but it was well above the waterline, and was patched and plugged rapidly enough. At six bells of the first watch, or what would have been six bells had there been any bells at all on *Nicodemus*, the man from the foretop came into the gun deck.

"What news?" I asked him.

"Damned cold, sir," he said. His hands were wrinkled and his face wind-burned. "I'm for my monkey jacket."

"What of *Alecto*?"

"Nothing but fog smoke," he said. "Can't see a thing." He put on his pea coat, replaced his oilskins, and returned to the deck.

From the private diary of Miss Columbia Abrams.

JUNE 21ST, 1863

I SHOULD WRITE DOWN ALL THAT I REMEMBER OF our battle with *Alecto*, before time can do its work upon the acts and feelings of memory, transforming them into an exhibition of sentimental tableaux— pleasant to look upon and fit for public show, but lacking the motion of life.

When night fell after the first day of our pursuit, I retired briefly to my cabin for a change of clothing, if bare skin underneath John Nevis's cloak can be so described. My own working uniform (for such, as regards purpose, was the seamless woolen robe that Captain Sharps had supplied) lay rain-soaked and abandoned on the deck above. I decided at the time that I quite envied Mr. Nevis his cloak, which was of heavy wool, lined with silk throughout; I only wished that I had thought to obtain something similar before leaving New York. My good winter cape was warm enough for the city, but not for standing on deck long hours in the freezing rain. For what I next intended, however, it would do.

I shut the cabin door long enough to strip off Mr. Nevis's cloak and wrap my own around my shoulders. Then I opened the door again and gave the lieutenant's cloak to the sailor who had escorted me to my cabin.

"Take this back to Mr. Nevis," I said. "With my thanks."

"Yes, ma'am," he said, and departed with his arms full of wet fabric.

As soon as he was gone, I wrapped my own cape more tightly around me—for I still wore nothing underneath—retrieved my key to the locked chamber, and made my way to the heart of *Nicodemus*. The Marines who guarded it were accustomed by now to my comings and goings at all hours and in all manner of dress, and allowed me to pass without question. Once alone inside the chamber, I let my cape fall to the floor and approached the glowing wooden sphere.

"*Nicodemus*," I said. "My dear friend. Are you well?"

I laid my hand against the wood, and felt awareness of the spirit's presence flood into me. The touch brought a modicum of reassurance—the ship had suffered no damage so far that could not be repaired, and the men working at the pumps kept the water in the hold from reaching a dangerous level—but I also felt a pressing awareness that something aboard ship was not right.

"We hunt *Alecto,* and are hunted in turn," I said. "That's bad enough for anyone, I think."

Nicodemus, I was given to understand, was not afraid of *Alecto.*

"Why should you be? Any destruction visited upon this ship means freedom for you. I would not blame you if I thought you hoped for our defeat."

Vehement denial. *Alecto* was a vile thing, an unnatural creation, growing hungrier the more it fed, and close already to overmastering those who thought they had mastered it. *Nicodemus* was in full accord with our desire that it should be stopped.

"Then it's victory or death for us," I said. "No middle ground. And if we lose, we'll be slaughtered to feed *Alecto's* hunger."

I did not speak aloud the rest of my thought—that I, as that rare and unnatural thing, a female aboard a ship of war, might well face an ordeal worse even than the sacrificial altar and the obsidian knife. But the knowledge of it ran like cold water in my veins, and I pressed my forehead against the smooth wood of the armillary sphere and shivered.

Nicodemus lacked the words to speak of encouragement and reassurance, but I felt the warmth of the spirit's goodwill nonetheless, and the sense that it would protect me—would protect all of those it regarded as its friends—for as long as the ship itself was able. What concerned *Nicodemus* at this time,

however, was not *Alecto* at all; not the killer somewhere out there in the ice and dark, but a much
closer danger.

"Show me, then," I said. "Give me something I can
warn Mr. Nevis or the captain about. I can't do anything to help if I can't see where the problem lies."

At once a press of images crowded into my head:
Captain Sharps keeping watch by his froglike compass-
idol, his life essence visible to *Nicodemus* as a cold
grey flame; the crew at their labors, burning in warm
red and yellow; and a few among them who did not
burn at all, only reflected a faint image of the captain's icy grey. The walking, working dead—*Nicodemus* did not like them, and the living crew feared
them. For a long time there had been Wharton and
Trask, after Portsmouth and after the Azores, but
now there were more, too many all at once for the
living men to deny what was before their eyes.

And *Alecto*—I pulled my hand away from the armillary sphere. "No. Show me no more of her, *Nicodemus*. I saw enough the last time to know her for
what she is."

I laid my hand again on the polished wood, and felt
apology and reassurance. No more pictures, then, of
Alecto in my mind; only the knowledge, presented
urgently, that someone aboard the Rebel ship was
not idle as they ran ahead of us out in the darkness.
Not all attacks require weapons, and an adversary
skilled in the metaphysical disciplines knows how to
bring pressure to bear against his enemy's weakest
point, be it mind or heart or soul.

Of a sudden, I knew what *Nicodemus* knew, and I was afraid. I did not need pictures in my mind to explain it further, when I had watched the progression of events with my own eyes. Time had proven the schoolteachers of my childhood right: our uncontrolled fancies can indeed act upon the universe. The crew's increasing resentment of Captain Sharps and distrust of his metaphysical learning, combined with their fear of *Alecto* and of the greater unknown, had opened wide a door through which our enemy's mystical attack could enter.

"The crew," I said. "Oh, God—*Alecto* will try to provoke them into mutiny. What am I to do, *Nicodemus*? What am I to do?"

Knowledge again flowed into me without words. One thing was possible. I could become a vessel for some portion of the spirit's power, freeing at least that part of it to act outside the constraints of the spells that bound it into the ship—if I trusted *Nicodemus*. And if *Nicodemus* could trust me, for the use and direction of that power would be under the control of my will, and not the spirit's.

"We are friends, *Nicodemus*," I said. "And friends trust one another. We'll do it together."

*The narrative of Lieutenant
John Nevis, USN, continued.*

I RETURNED TO THE MAIN DECK TO FIND THAT THE storm had somewhat abated, at least as far as rain, though the seas were still high and the wind still blowing a gale. I was grateful for the woolen boat cloak that Miss Adams had returned to me. *Nicodemus* had been driving steadily onward at tremendous speed for nigh on four-and-twenty hours without slacking, and a moment's internal calculation informed me that we must by now be well below thirty degrees south of the equator. Our pursuit of *Alecto* had brought us down into the Roaring Forties, where the westerly winds blow night and day intemperately over the ocean's vast expanse.

The morning fog showed no sign of burning away, being suffused instead with a sickly, pinkish light, through which the black masts and lines of our own vessel were so blurred and obscured that from the wheel I could not make out the bow. The mist that surrounded us was full of sounds: low

mutterings and high-pitched far-off cries; a thrumming as of a distant chant; a drumbeat, almost too
faint to be heard. I told myself that it was ice moving about in the freezing water.

Lieutenant Vincent approached me a little while
after I came on deck, carefully holding on to lines
and railings to maintain his footing. I could tell
from his overbright eyes and unshaven cheeks that
he had slept no more than I.

"Listen," he said to me.

"To what?" I asked.

"Behind the wind," he said. "The grumbling. Do
you hear it? It sounds like words—I feel I can almost make them out."

I paused. The sounds in the fog had not gone
away. "Very like voices," I said. "But I suppose there
is some natural cause."

"Oh, belike," he replied, but with a weight of sar-
casm in his voice. "Natural causes are the first I find
wherever I look upon this ship."

A moment later, I heard a confused jumble of
noise, just before the main companionway from below burst into a swarm of activity. Amidst flailing
bodies and the shouts of men, the sailors burst forth,
pushing and manhandling ahead of them their
comrades, the dead who now walked, and propel-
ling those late unfortunates toward the rail. The
wind shrieked and the waters roared as, with a sullen plunge, each of the unburied dead was thrown
over the side.

Then Hopkins—he who earlier had been struck

dumb for protesting the lack of ceremonial when we crossed the Line—rose from the fray and headed aft toward us at a run. His eyes were wild and affrighted, rolling about wildly like those of a panicked horse, and his mouth worked without sound so that he appeared to me as one under some species of compulsion. The seamen who followed close behind him exhibited the same mindless frenzy. Hopkins laid hands on Lieutenant Vincent, and he and his messmates began to wrestle him toward the rail.

"Gunner!" said I, "Help me!" as I hastened to the lieutenant's defense. Alas that pistols and swords were not to be had on this ship!

Aid came then not from Gunner Bellevue, but from another quarter. Froggie's arm, which had for a long time lain dead forward, spun to the right, and the helmsman—who by God's grace had remained so far untouched by the madness that had afflicted his shipmates—put the wheel hard over in an attempt to follow the idol's guidance. *Nicodemus* heeled over at such an extreme angle that her yardends nearly touched the confused seas, and I was able to look out across the deck and see the ocean below me. Pallid ovals in the water marked the faces of the men who had been thrown overboard; now they floated, and all about them spun the fins of sharks.

So, too, did the sharks follow *Alecto*, who depended upon the blood and hearts of living men for her unnatural existence. The dead men of our boarding party had only come sooner than the rest of us to what would be our ultimate grave, should we fail to prove victorious in our struggle with the Rebel.

As if the thought itself had conjured her, the black shape of that accursed ship appeared without warning in the fog to our starboard side, drifting silently while the mist around us muttered with half-heard voices and the wind screamed in our rigging.

"Men," I shouted. "To your guns!"—not knowing if they would heed, but fervent in my hope that the well-drilled fighting spirit of the American bluejacket would prove strong enough to overmaster the sudden madness that had beset them.

"I can't hold her," the helmsman sang out. "Bear a hand!"

My men, the gun crews, halted and gazed about wildly, as though torn between blind compulsion and obedience to the order that might save all their lives. I felt my heart sink within me when it seemed for a moment that they would not obey. For a moment only—then one of the sailors left the press of men at the side and went to stand beside the helmsman, and put his back into turning and holding the ship's wheel.

Froggie's arm, meanwhile, had swung completely about. The water boiled white where we had passed, and the wind, which had been blowing from the port quarter, had gone from dead astern to ahead, and was now again on the port quarter as we went.

A moment later, Captain Sharps came up from below decks, with Lieutenant Dodge following, and ordered, "Beat to quarters!"

"She's turning more smartly than we," Lieutenant Dodge said. He pointed back at *Alecto*, for that ship was coming up astern of us, where, lacking a stern chaser, we could not bring guns to bear. *Alecto*, suffering no such lack, seemed intent on bringing her bow chaser into range the fastest way.

Captain Sharps glared at the press of men still gathered near the rail. "All of you, to your stations!"

The mute Hopkins, who had been standing with the others by the rail, stood away and struck Captain Sharps with a fid that he had by a lanyard about his wrist, knocking the captain down onto the deck. Lieutenant Dodge reached the captain's side at the same time as the master-at-arms struck Hopkins with his fist, doubling him over.

In that very instant, Columbia Abrams appeared at the after companionway, arising from below decks like Venus new-raised from the sea, and in the same state of nature. Her dark hair blew about her shoulders as if stirred by a life of its own, her eyes flashed, and she appeared limned from head to toe in golden light. No man could bear to look upon her as she paced through the crowd to where the drama was taking place upon the quarterdeck; rather, they all hastened to their appointed stations, the madness that had overshadowed them driven away by the brightness of her passing.

"Mr. Nevis, see to the captain," she said. Then she

reached out her hand and laid it on Hopkins. He cried out and fell to the deck senseless.

"Master at Arms," she said quietly, "take him below. He is not in his right mind." Then, to Lieutenant Dodge: "Sir, I suggest that we do not wish to make contact with that vessel."

Lieutenant Dodge glanced astern at *Alecto.* "Speed," he said at once. "Make all speed possible," and the helmsman spun the trick wheel forward to the stops.

Lieutenant Dodge gave orders to place the seas on the quarter, lest we be pooped, and again ordered speed. But before he could do more, Captain Sharps rose from where he had fallen under Hopkins's blow and strode over to where the master-at-arms was preparing to haul the unconscious man below.

"Leave that man be," the captain said.

He stepped up to the stricken Hopkins, seized the man by the throat, and dragged him to his feet. Then he walked Hopkins back to the stern rail.

"Look away aft," Captain Sharps commanded. "Tell me what you see. Speak."

"A ship," Hopkins said. His voice creaked like a door hinge gone cracked and rusty from disuse.

"Look again," the captain said. "What do you see?"

"Death." His voice was now closer to a shriek.

"Yes," Captain Sharps said. "Death pursues us. I alone can save you. We have come all this distance to fight death; now—begone from my sight."

And with that he cast the man away from him onto the deck.

Through it all *Nicodemus* shuddered as she cut the waves, pitching up then slamming forward and down, only to shudder to a halt at the bottom of each trough.

Fast we fled, and fast *Alecto* followed. I instructed one of my gun crews to unship a cannon from its place last in the rank on the port side and jury-rig it aft, pointing out toward the Rebel's pursuing shape. Astern of us, I could see the ghostly shapes of dead men's faces in the water, the members of *Nicodemus*'s boarding party following still the ship on which they had labored when alive, and from which they had gone into the deep. And always Froggie pointed dead astern, and *Alecto* trailed us as if she were under tow.

"At least the Rebels aren't gaining on us," Gunner Bellevue said.

"No," I said. "I fancy not."

"What do you reckon our speed to be, sir?"

I shook my head. "In excess of thirty knots, I would say. Perhaps twice that—the log line broke at twenty-four."

A flash of light came from *Alecto*, but not from the discharge of a cannon. Rather was it like lightning striking upward from the ship's deck toward her mastheads.

"What new deviltry is this, sir?" Bellevue wondered aloud.

"I don't know," I said. "But I don't like it."

"Johnny," Captain Sharps said. "You have your chaser rigged—stand by to fire as soon as we're steady."

He gave a series of orders to the helm. *Nicodemus* responded by matching speed with the wind, so that we seemed then to be at the center of a dead calm, even though the wind around us whipped the sea to foam, and the white water of our passage boiled astern of us and flew away in arcs from our bows.

"A clever trick," I said to Bellevue. "Let us assay to fire."

Alas, the powder was wet. Then began the tedious process of worming out the ball and the charge. The captain meanwhile paced the deck, wearing his bizarre fighting uniform. He laid his hand on Froggie's head for a moment, then resumed pacing.

The air around us had grown distinctly colder during the chase so far, so that our breath steamed.

At length we had the barrel cleared in our improvised stern chaser. Now began the process of firing ball after ball at the Rebel, each shot as carefully laid as ever I could make it. While this was going on—since idle hands are the devil's playground, and I wanted no chance for thoughts of mutiny to recur—I brought up the rest of the men in my division to worm out the guns in the starboard battery, in order to give the ammunition loaded in them to the single barrel that bore on *Alecto*.

So we passed the morning, into the day watch;

and while some of our balls hit the Rebel, and others appeared not to do so, yet no damage appeared on our opponent. I became convinced that they had upon their ship protection similar to that which we ourselves had so far enjoyed thanks to Miss Abrams's good offices. At length we were reduced to enough shot for two broadsides, and then to one. The powder supply was equally short.

"One more broadside and our day'll be over," the gunner said. "We'll be naught but a lugger then."

"We'll see," quoth Captain Sharps. He ordered, "Slow the ship!", and the helmsman unloosed the trick wheel and spun it rapidly back.

"Sir," Lieutenant Dodge protested. "The Rebel still comes on apace."

On and on came *Alecto*. She was close enough to count the links on her fore-chains when Captain Sharps raised his hands on high and cried aloud in a foreign tongue, and the lightning that had before risen from *Alecto*'s deck came down now from the clouds above and struck her masts. St. Elmo's fire played about our own yard-ends, and sparkling sheets of fire flashed from *Alecto*'s silver masts.

But while from that point on she drew no closer, still she did not slow.

*The Narrative of Lieutenant
John Nevis, USN, continued.*

THE DAY DREW ON. *ALECTO* STAYED ALWAYS astern of us, a dark shape in the fog, so well-matched in speed to *Nicodemus* that the gap between us neither closed so much as would give the Rebel a certain shot, nor widened enough to let us alter course and slip away. As we had done the day before, and all during the night, we ran ever southward through the Roaring Forties—only now we were the pursued, and not the pursuer.

The rain abated somewhat by midday, though never so much that *Alecto* ceased to be shrouded in mist, and the air grew steadily colder. The madness that had earlier seized the crew did not return, but their temper remained unhappy and restless. Nor can I say that my own spirits were much the steadier. The chill air, the grey light, the half-heard noises in the fog—whispering as much in the mind as in the ear—all combined to lowering effect. The white ovals of dead men's faces glimmered continually in the water astern, half seen from the corners of one's eyes.

Mr. Dodge, Mr. Vincent, and I kept up a desultory flow of conversation, as much to preserve the appearance of calm as for any other reason; to this day I recall little of what was said, other than that it was all of the most commonplace nature imaginable. Young Mr. Bash, being the supply officer, had gone below, in order to commence an inventory of those ship's stores that had not been hurt by water in the storm; Miss Abrams had retired belowdecks at the same time, presumably to attend to her duties there.

Captain Sharps, meanwhile, paced back and forth on the deck without speaking, never more than an arm's reach from Froggie. His eyes were very bright, almost feverish. Abruptly, at three bells of the noon watch, he seemed to come back into himself.

"Put the rudder over hard to lee," he ordered.

"Aye aye, sir," said the helmsman, and complied.

No sooner had he done so than *Nicodemus* began to spin rapidly in the ocean, causing the dim grey shape that was *Alecto* to become first darker, then solid—then, as our stem bore down upon her, she turned once again and raced over the ocean directly at us, as if desirous of colliding head-to-head.

By now Captain Sharps had taken his accustomed place in the rigging, but Miss Abrams was nowhere to be seen. After the events of the morning, we had not yet mustered another boarding party, nor did handing weapons to the sailors at that moment seem wise. None of the officers remaining on deck dared go forward, lest their actions spur the men once again into madness.

"It's a long way to swim home," Lieutenant Dodge said. "We sink ourselves, as is likely, and . . ." He shook his head. "At least we'll have tried."

The two ships meanwhile drew near to one another—then, like two great magnets of similar poles, they sprang apart, throwing up tall fans and plumes of white water as they did so. *Alecto* passed close aboard down our starboard side, yet without firing her guns. Perhaps, I thought, the Rebels too were reduced to hoarding their shot; perhaps they too were surprised; perhaps their guns were not loaded; perhaps their powder was wet throughout.

As *Alecto* passed starboard to starboard down our side, Captain Sharps cried out in a loud voice in a language that I did not know—neither Latin nor Greek, nor French nor German—and opened his right hand to the heavens as if cupping a substance that none could see.

The mastheads and yards of *Alecto* glowed blue, and red fire flew from Captain Sharps's hand toward that vessel. Sparks like lightning darted from mast to spar on the Rebel sloop. Thunder rolled.

Again the captain cried out in that unknown tongue, and again the thunder rang as lightning flew from his fingertips.

The electric fire splashed over our opponent and the water around the Rebel ship burned with reflected color. The rain that had been falling steadily once more increased in strength, and the fog thickened. White flakes of snow, fat and cold, hurtled through the air amidst the rain; then sleet, that stung and burned.

"Why won't he show himself?" Captain Sharps demanded of the air around him. "Why won't the bastard show himself?"

He did not seem to expect an answer, at least not from me, nor did I give one.

Alecto turned toward us—and once again, just as a collision seemed imminent, we sprang apart. Then she was gone, vanished into the fog and the falling snow, and the sky above us darkened as we ran before the storm.

Froggie sat on his tripod, his arm moving first right, then left, now quickly, now slowly. The helmsman could not keep it centered, neither forward nor aft.

"No matter," Captain Sharps said, as the last of the light faded. "Lash the wheel midships. Go below. Take food and drink. I will remain on watch. All of you, go!"

On that order, I retreated below to my bunk and, discarding only my cloak, turned in all standing— happy to be out of the weather, but greatly distressed by all that I had seen.

The night was long but untroubled. The pounding of the ship through mountainous seas was steady. Hard as sleeping was, exhaustion took the men, the other officers, and me. Whether the captain slept, or Miss Abrams, I do not know.

I awoke some time later to find that the ship's uneasy motion had ceased. The yellow lantern-glow cast strange highlights onto the inner bulkheads, where ice crystals glistened on the wood, and for a moment, before my mind cleared, I imagined myself at the shipyard back in Thule. I pulled on my coat, my breath steaming, and made my way to the main deck.

There I found the other officers gathered on the quarterdeck. The night was dark, but it was a darkness shot through with lurid cold fire, blue and green, coming from everywhere and nowhere at once, but not so bright as to cast a shadow.

"Have you slept?" Mr. Dodge asked.

"I have."

"Then you're one of the lucky few," he told me. "Take the deck."

"Sir. Where is the captain?"

In answer, Lieutenant Dodge pointed to the quarter, where Captain Sharps crouched, his knees drawn up and his arms around his legs, staring at Froggie.

"He won't speak," Lieutenant Dodge said.

"What injury or sickness of the mind is this?" I asked. "How long has he been thus?"

"Since I came on deck during the midwatch and found him so. If he does not return to himself soon, I intend to make for the nearest friendly port."

"That won't be easy, in a ship with neither chronometer nor compass."

"We have a copy of Bowditch, we have charts,

and when the fog clears, we have the stars. Odysseus plowed the seas with less."

"Odysseus also took ten years to return to his home," I pointed out.

"And eight of those years he spent living at ease on Calypso's island—by which we may know that he was a true sailor, and nobody's fool." Dodge slapped me on the shoulder. "With luck, we shall face neither Scylla nor Charybdis. Now, turn to."

I looked over the ship's side. Lumps and bits of half-frozen ice slid by us as we made bare steerageway through the glowing mist. The sounds of men chanting in the distance remained, mingled with what could have been distant shouts and the roaring of beasts. The faces of the dead men followed us still.

"The noise is only the ice grinding," said Mr. Bash, who had come up to join the rest of us on deck. I do not think he believed it himself.

Froggie was behaving oddly. The pointer arm was circling, endlessly circling. What had been our compass was such no longer. I thought perhaps the idol's failure had proved the stroke that unhinged the captain's mind—or perhaps, in this case, cause and effect had run the other way.

"Do you suppose *Alecto* is moving thus?" I wondered aloud, and nodded toward the idol.

"Sharks move like that," Bash said, "as they approach the pitiful drowned. And our own case is not much better."

"Such speculation is unhelpful."

It was the captain's voice. Startled, I turned in time to see him rising stiffly to his feet.

"I have traveled far this night," he continued, "and I see now the way of it. The spirit of water shall do my will."

Mr. Dodge appeared amazed by this statement. "Captain, do you think it wise? The crew—"

"—shall all be hanged. Fetch Miss Abrams to my quarters."

Froggie's arm paused in its endless circling, and fixed two points on the starboard.

"Turn toward!" Captain Sharps ordered, all his previous lassitude vanished in an instant. "Lay me alongside the Rebel. Put over grapnels if you can. Put a broadside into their timbers from the range of a handspike; see if they can hold against that!"

"Sir," I said, for it seemed to me that we were *in extremis*, and no other word came to me.

A rumble of thunder sounded ahead, a broadside from our unseen foe.

"So much for them being out of shot," said Lieutenant Vincent.

"How can they see to shoot?" asked Bash.

"They're as blind as we are," I said. "And as mad."

With a cracking sound, a ball took one of our spars near the main truck. The deck was instantly littered with splinters of wood and knife-sharp scraps of obsidian, for the ball had shattered when it hit.

"Perhaps not so blind," said Vincent.

"Beat to quarters," the captain ordered; "run out the guns. We know our situation but they do not. They must suppose us to be a dog with teeth yet."

I went forward to see to the gun crews. The port side was clear. I stood up on the rail in order to look better into the mist. It was growing lighter. Somewhere beyond the fog, the sun had risen.

Then came the cry from the masthead, "Ship ahoy, broad on the starboard bow!"

And so it was, a darker shape, not a half-mile off. Light flashed down her side as she pulled her broadside.

"Hard right! More speed!" Captain Sharps cried out.

He's trying to engage *Alecto* to port, thought I. A neat bit of shiphandling, but that won't be enough to save us.

The wind of our passage was shrieking, and spray leapt up to either side. Chunks of floating ice struck our stempost with thumps that I could feel through the deck. And now Miss Abrams appeared to take her battle station. She was shivering visibly, and even from half the length of the deck away I could see that she had not slept and was perishing of fatigue.

Alecto fired again from a cable's length, raking us as we turned. Miss Abrams cried out; in the same moment a ball from *Alecto* struck Froggie squarely on. The obsidian shot and the wooden idol vanished together in splinters and shards, and those officers gathered by him on the quarterdeck, the captain and all, fell as if cut down with a scythe. A pink mist of blood rose, mingled with the white of the fog, and was blown astern.

Even as they fell, *Nicodemus* came to a stop in the ocean, as rapidly as if a sea anchor had been cast astern. We turned broadside into the swells under influence of wind and water, and began to roll.

Alecto vanished like a wraith into the mist.

The Narrative of Lieutenant
John Nevis, USN, continued.

AT THE VERY MOMENT THE BALL STRUCK AFT,
Wharton and Trask, who had pulled the lines for so
many days without speaking, still without speaking fell to the deck, and at once assumed the foul
and corrupted aspect of men who had lain dead for
weeks. *Nicodemus* came to a halt in the sea, while
our nemesis circled us steadily, by turns hidden in
the mist and revealed by the flashes of her guns.

The woeful fog still surrounded us, enwrapping
the ship and flowing into every opening of my garments. I had thought myself acclimated to cold after
the sojourn at Thule, so recent yet by the rush of
events driven so far from memory, but I was wrong.
The air in these waters was colder still.

"Sir," said Ensign Bash. He was speaking very
loudly, I noticed, as though he had been deafened
by a nearby pistol shot. "Captain. What are your
orders, sir?"

My mind caught on the unfamiliar word—unfamiliar, at least, in its present context. " 'Captain?' "

"You are the senior survivor, sir. What are your orders?"

"I cannot shoot lightning bolts from my fingers," I said.

"Do you intend to ask for quarter?"

"No," I said. That much, at least, I was certain of. We were undermanned and outgunned, but better to go down fighting than be taken to feed *Alecto*'s unceasing hunger. "Full sail. See what weapons, if any, are to be found aboard this ship, and issue them to the crew."

A soft hand slipped into mine, from behind. "Come with me, John," said Miss Abrams. "There is something I wish to show you."

"What thing?"

"As captain, you must know. The heart of *Nicodemus*."

I threw my boat cloak around her shoulders. She was all gooseflesh and shivering heavily in the frigid air. She smiled and bobbed her head in thanks.

"Quickly," she said. "Soon their shot will find us."

"Why have they not approached?" Mr. Bash asked me.

"I expect they anticipate some trick," I said. "When they realize we are helpless—"

"Not so helpless, perhaps," Miss Abrams said. She darted aft, paused to search for something in the pocket of Captain Sharps's robe, then hurried on past the scene of carnage to the after companion-way, her hand stained with blood. I followed. She was made of stern stuff, this young woman.

The two Marines who guarded the entrance to the spar deck blocked my path. "I'm afraid you can't go in there, sir," said the senior of the two. "Captain's orders."

"Stand aside," Miss Abrams said. "Mr. Nevis is captain now."

Discipline held firm. The Marines voiced no dismay or disbelief; but they were not ignorant as to what extremity of disaster Miss Abrams's words implied, and their faces showed it. The senior man said only, "Orders, sir?"

"Go topside," I said. "Prepare to repel boarders."

"Yes, sir." They saluted and departed.

Miss Abrams, meanwhile, had a key clutched in her hand. She turned it in the lock and opened the door and went forward. Again, I followed her.

"Captain," she said. "There is something very important that we have to do."

I scarcely heard her. I was gazing, amazed, at the wonders before me. In the center of the space stood an instrument of dark wood and blue light—an armillary sphere the height of a man, wholly surrounded by a net of lines, sheaves, and blocks. Balls of cast iron depended from the network at points variously closer to and farther from the central sphere; I judged that the lines and tackle served to alter the positions of the iron balls according to need.

It was a pity, I thought, that Mr. Cromwell was dead. I should have liked to hear the engineering officer's explanation of the mechanism and its function.

The air in the space was oddly charged, tickling across my exposed skin even though there was no breeze. I considered how Miss Abrams, in her state of undress, must be affected by the sensation, and found the thought sufficiently disturbing that I turned my attention back in haste to the glowing sphere.

I drew breath and mastered my voice with some difficulty. "What in the name of God is that?"

"It is in God's name that we must proceed now," Miss Abrams said. "We spoke before of *Nicodemus* having been designed from the beginning to house a captive spirit."

"I remember."

"That sphere—the heart of *Nicodemus*—is its prison. Break the sphere, and the spirit goes free."

A crashing sound came from above, and the deck shivered beneath my feet.

"That may be so," said I; "but we are in desperate straits, and yonder imprisoned spirit, if my understanding does not fail me, is the source of all our motive power."

"Good cannot come of evil," she said. "Do you think we can win against an enslaving power by holding another power in slavery?"

"And what will happen if we let it go?" I demanded. "Will the spirit that was *Nicodemus* help us out of the goodness of its heart, or will it seek revenge on its late captors?"

"It longs to be free. But it hates *Alecto* even more." Her cheeks colored a little. "And—as do I, John Nevis—it thinks kindly of you."

Captain Sharps had trusted Miss Abrams's communion with the ship's inhabiting spirit, I thought. I could do no less.

"Very well," I said. "I'll have the ship's carpenter take an axe to the thing straightway. That should do the trick."

Her cheeks reddened still further. "An axe won't work. The bonds that hold the spirit tied to *Nicodemus* are not mechanical, but metaphysical. Only one who is *virgo intacta*—untouched and unbroken—can lay hands on the sphere."

"Young woman," I said. "Miss Abrams—"

"There *is* no other way. I have worked with the sphere and cared for it since leaving Thule; the bonds between me and it are strong. And the spirit . . . the spirit is with me now also." She was blushing furiously now, and not on her face alone. "Change me, and the bonds between spirit and ship change likewise."

"Miss Abrams," I said again. My voice thickened and choked with emotions too strong to easily describe. "Columbia. I cannot ask such a sacrifice of you. I cannot."

"Then *Alecto* takes us all. And the souls of all those she takes afterward will be on our heads, because we could have stopped her, and failed at the last."

She was magnificent in her resolution. I was inspired then with an equal resolve.

"Miss Abrams," I said, "I am the captain of this ship, and have the authority to solemnize marriages aboard her. Will you do me the honor of becoming my wife?"

"Mr. Nevis," she said, "I will."

"Then I now pronounce us man and wife."

From above came another crash of shot hitting the side, this time mingled with cries of pain and dismay.

"We should make haste," she said.

From the private diary
of Miss Columbia Abrams.

JUNE 21ST, 1863

WHAT PASSED BETWEEN LIEUTENANT JOHN NEVIS, myself, and the spirit of *Nicodemus* was not completely a surprise. One cannot attend a girls' college for four years, living in the dormitories all during that time, without hearing a great deal of discussion and speculation on the matter.

Books that touched factually on the subject tended to be in Latin, which produced in some of us the motive to attain mastery of that tongue; and Latin poetry, while greatly inflaming to the senses, provided few details of the mechanics. A novel printed in French—unedifying in its literary merits, but nevertheless greatly sought—had passed surreptitiously from hand to hand, and an illustrated anatomy text lay under lock and key in the college library, its perusal limited to certain advanced students in natural philosophy (among whom I myself was counted). The terms used therein did not match those in the novel, nor were the cross-sections entirely ideal to satisfy curiosity.

Much silliness, therefore, passed back and forth among us, in conversations late at night beneath wards of secrecy—but when I look back, I see that out of all our shared gossip and misinformation, we contrived to distill at least the essential truth.

I would not have known what to say or how to begin, however, if it had not been for *Nicodemus*. The portion of the ship's spirit that I had carried with me up onto the deck and used to quell the mutineers still moved within me, and *Nicodemus* was older, and wiser, and more shameless than I. It urged me on.

I met Lieutenant Nevis's eyes—it was difficult, even with the wooden bands and rings of the armillary sphere a solid, reassuring presence at my back— and said, "It is necessary that we perform the marriage act. And I have the advantage of you here, John. You are still clothed, whilst I am not."

"You have it in your power to alter that," he said. His voice was rough, and little more than a whisper.

"Yes." My own voice was steady—mine, or that of *Nicodemus* speaking through me, I could not tell. "So much as is necessary."

"Do it," he said. "Please."

I must confess that I giggled then, like the schoolgirl I had been, and whispered, "Thou art as innocent as I!"

He reddened. "I had hoped to bring my virginity to my wedding night."

"And so you have," I whispered, kissing him.

Carefully, as though reaching out to a wild animal that might at any moment take fright and vanish, I began to unbutton the front of his trousers. I had never touched a man before in so intimate a manner, and the sensations I experienced upon doing so left me thankful for the support of the wooden sphere at my back. Mr. Nevis placed his hand lightly on my hip; no other man had ever touched me thus. I nearly swooned, and blushed all over.

The last of the buttons slipped free of its buttonhole. John bit his lip and stood trembling. "For the love of God, Miss Abrams—"

"Columbia," I said. My hands found cotton drawers and more buttons; I worked even more carefully than before.

"For the love of God, Columbia—don't stop now."

"Oh, John. I shall not. There."

Things I had heard in the dark and not understood became clear to me in *Nicodemus*'s light, and the thing that I most wanted and that which would break the spirit free of its prison were one and the same.

"Now, John," I said. "Quickly, oh quickly, and do not hold back."

I braced my back against the wooden cage that held *Nicodemus*, and John pressed his hands against it to either side of me, and we became one, as though meant to be so from the beginning of time.

*The narrative of Lieutenant
John Nevis, USN, continued.*

WITH A GROAN AND SNAP OF RENDING TIMBER, the great sphere split in two from top to bottom. Light burst out of the broken pieces, a dazzling brilliance that outdid the earlier illumination as the tropic sun outshines the distant stars—burning, splitting into sparks, rising and swirling and coalescing into glowing clouds that shifted from blue to green, then back to blue again. I felt a tingling sensation beginning in my feet and hands, where they touched the deck and the remnants of the wooden sphere, and in short order suffusing my entire body. Perhaps now I *could* shoot lightning bolts from my fingers.

"On deck," I said to Columbia, as soon as the power of speech was mine again. "We have much to do."

"Yes, John," she said, and—slipping her warm hand into mine—followed me away from the wreckage of Captain Sharps's mystical device.

Above decks, much had changed. The fog had dissipated, blown to tatters by a fresh wind; the sun was a sullen yellow disk low on the horizon, burning through the clouds. All the sea about us was filled with ice, massive blocks higher than the masts, glittering like diamonds.

Broad on our port beam and presenting her port aspect, *Alecto* made a dark, predatory shape amongst the icebergs. Her course was a hundred and eighty degrees away from *Nicodemus*, and we were closer to her than we had ever been before in daylight. I could see her deck clearly, where a man in a yellow robe and a crown of jade and feathers stood beside that queer pyramid, with a bloody knife in his hand and blood flowing unchecked from her scuppers.

"Behold the abomination," Columbia said, in tones carrying enough to be heard by all on deck. "It is a loathsome thing, and fit only for destruction."

"Yes, ma'am," said Gunner Bellevue. He seemed frightened by her presence—as I might have been, before the act of marriage made us one, to see how the spirit within her made her whole body appear to shine with an inner light. He turned to me with relief on his features. "She's loading her guns for another broadside, sir."

"There are iron cannonballs below," I said to him. "On the third deck, in the engineering space. Cut them free of their lines, and bring them up. Double-load to port, iron and brass in each gun."

The gun crews of *Alecto*, meanwhile, were working their swabs and ramrods, but slowly, while our two ships drifted a bit apart. The long chase through cold and foul weather had weakened the enemy as much as us; and if there were any decent men among them, the fearful nature of the ship they sailed in must have weighed on them like stone.

For my part, despite the danger in which we then stood, I had seldom felt so light of heart as I did at that moment. I felt the deck of *Nicodemus* thrilling beneath my feet, and I was aware in my own body of every plank of her, every peg, every line, every ballast stone. There was no question in my mind any longer; I knew what we needed to do.

The narrative of Lieutenant John Nevis, USN, continued.

"NICODEMUS," I CRIED ALOUD, GESTURING TO-ward *Alecto*, "bring me portside to below her stern!" Then, to the boatswain, "Pipe boarding party—and handsomely!"

He saluted and ran forward, piping the call. We came left rapidly, but as we did so, *Alecto* came left as well. We turned, and she turned with us, our speeds well matched. As she turned, she came below our port battery, and my gun crews, loyal men all, fired as one, and our double-loaded guns sent iron and brass into her timbers; nor was she warded now, and I could see the damage to her planks and frames.

No sooner had the smoke cleared from our final broadside than a ripple appeared in the flat calm of that oily, ice-choked sea. The ripple became a whirl-pool, opening up between *Nicodemus* and *Alecto*. Larger and larger it grew, like a gaping maw. An ice floe tilted into it, and swirled about. The whirlpool expanded, sucking in bergy bits and growlers, until the rim of it reached the sides of our two ships simultaneously—whereupon both tilted over and commenced chasing one another around and around the glass-green walls of the whirlpool at a fearful speed.

The sky was now on our starboard beam. Looking over the port side I saw the swirling water descending to foam far away beneath us. The wind howled through our rigging, and the rapidity of our passage held us for a moment steady in the maelstrom. Then we slipped lower, and *Alecto* was at once dead ahead of us and dead astern.

More ice slipped into the whirlpool, in larger and larger chunks, and was sucked down ahead of us, descending those steep sides faster than we were proceeding. *Alecto* was before us, behind us, and directly above us; we could look straight up and see their deck, as they could look down on ours, and the funnel that held us grew ever more narrow. Our two ships drew closer and closer together, until we were near enough that I could see the men on *Alecto* struggling with her helm, and mark the fear and desperation on their features. Soon, I thought, their masts and ours must touch.

All at once the Rebel came hard left, so that her bow pointed directly downward into the pit of blackness, spray, and grinding ice that marked the bottom of the maelstrom. She shot away from us, and without my order *Nicodemus* wrenched hard left to follow. Now we were sailing straight down toward the center of the earth, through a tunnel made entirely of frothing water.

"Your orders, sir?" It was Mr. Bash again. His countenance was pale, his eyes were wide and dark, but his voice, pitched to carry over the sound of the waters, remained steady. He was wasted on the supply corps, I thought. Something to talk with him about later, if a "later" were vouchsafed to us.

"A ration of grog to every man," I said. "A double ration. Those who are of a mind to pray are encouraged to do so."

Alecto drove on and downward, with *Nicodemus* in close pursuit. White water foamed and flew away from us to either side like outspread wings, and the maelstrom roared in our ears like unremitting thunder. The sky was a small patch of blue, a circle far astern of us with the sun a brilliant dot in its center. The cold was extreme. I put my arm around Columbia's shoulder and pulled her close.

"It's good to be married," she said.

"Indeed," I said, and the blackness took us.

I felt Columbia press herself against me, and for an indefinite length of time I knew nothing further.

Letter from William Fowler, Able Seaman, aboard USS Nicodemus, to his sister Margaret Chapman of Marblehead, Massachusetts.

MY DEAREST SISTER MARGARET,

I write to you once again, in the hope that you will be comforted that I still live, despite what further scenes from this extraordinary voyage may have been revealed to you through your arts. My dearest sister, I am scarcely able myself to credit my survival, for I had been certain to have perished or worse many times in the days just past, nor did yesterday's dawn give me hope to see that sun's set.

We are commanded now by Mr. Nevis, a fine officer who seems much the sailors' friend. He speaks softly, yet with decision, so that all trust to his judgment and hasten to obey his commands. We before the mast are all well pleased by this event. Captain Sharps, of whom I have written before, is dead in a great battle we had of late with a Confederate pirate, and many more besides, but we carried the day as you will perceive.

It happened in that battle, when the captain was slain, that Lieutenant Nevis assumed command, not hesitating or faltering, but with a steadfast eye. And he sought me out amidst the smoke and the cannons' roar and addressed me by name, saying, "I understand that you have been below by the lazaret," to which I answered in the affirmative.

"Take your knife below," said he. "Go to that space of which we are both aware, and cut to pieces all the line that you find there. Bring the severed parts topside, and cast them over the rail."

I saluted and replied, "Aye aye!" as he turned to other concerns, for we were in that moment hard-pressed.

Then I went below, to find the Marine guards no longer at their post (I learned later that they had been reassigned to the tops, there to provide rifle fire to cover our boarding party should the need for one arise). Forward I went, into that chamber which I wrote to you of before, carrying a lantern that I took up on my way. I soon discovered, however, that no lantern was needed, for the entire third deck was filled with flitting points of light.

Like the fireflies of a summer's evening, they darted hither and thither. The massive wooden structure of interlocking rings and spheres, which I had marveled at on my previous visit, had been rent asunder by some unknown force, and lay in ruins on the deck. All about it, the lines lay slack, some of them hanging loose from the sheaves, others fallen onto the deck. I seized the nearest line, and turned to.

I commenced to cutting, and as I did so, I could hear a sound like a loud wind blowing. I dropped the severed part, seized anew the bitter end, and cut once more. The light around me grew brighter as the air grew thicker with the flickering lights, and the sound of wind grew ever louder.

And so I went, up and down the long space, cutting the lines again and again, each half fathom or full fathom as I guess. While I worked, the gunners' mates came to carry away those iron balls that had depended from the lines, as soon as I cut them free. I worked, and about my feet the brightness gathered, the separate lights multiplying and blending into a flowing stream, so like to clear water glimmering beneath the sun that I was like to gasp in amaze.

When I had cut free as many fathom lengths of line as I could carry in my arms, I gathered them up and ascended the ladder to the quarterdeck. There I cast my burden over the side to lee, then returned below. Three times I made this circuit, and three times cast away my burden, and each time the sound of wind belowdecks grew louder.

At length I was done, the light died below, the fireflies departed, the space was dark.

I went topside, and reported to the bosun that I was in need of a task, and he said, "Pray."

This I did, and most humbly, thinking of you and

Mother and Father, and beseeching Our Dear Lord and Savior, that I and my messmates might return in safety to shore.

I remained on my knees thus, as the light grew dark, then at once blazing light struck my cheeks and eyelids, and I looked about; and cried aloud, "Thanks be to Thee, my Lord, for Thy great mercy."

I shall tell you more on my return.

Your devoted brother,
Will

From the private diary of Miss Columbia Abrams.

JUNE 21ST, 1863

ALECTO PLUNGED INTO THE DEPTHS OF THE maelstrom with *Nicodemus* hot in pursuit. My experiences within the maelstrom were unique; nor have I shared them with any man; nor has any who went into the wild water shared similar visions with me.

Briefly, what happened is this: The roar of the waters filled my ears as I stood within my husband's embrace, and a haze passed across my vision. The haze cleared, and there was silence.

I stood alone in a long tunnel made of water, its sides and top arched, its bottom flat. I was walking on the water, garbed once more in the woolen robes which had been provided for me at the beginning of this endeavor, and all about me was dark, save for the end of the tunnel ahead, which was of a brilliant light never seen before on land or sea. The walls of the tunnel were smooth in the reflected light, but I did not touch them.

Then, without awareness of having left the tunnel, I found myself walking on a level plain that stretched out in all directions to a flat horizon. The pure brilliance that had dazzled my eyes a moment earlier was gone as if it had never been. The sky above me was all a mass of lowering clouds, and the horizon was limned in bilious light not strong enough to cast a shadow.

The ground beneath me was firm, not water but earth, and barren. A distant wind stirred the small hairs on the back of my neck and sent a shiver down my limbs. I recognized the light that seeped around the edges of the clouds. It was the light of fire.

Far away to my right a creature was moving— hunting for me, smelling for my blood.

My robes were with me still, and I wore sandals on my feet. In my left hand I held a flag on a tall staff, the banner of the Union. I turned toward the distant creature, ran toward it. My sandals slapped the earth as I ran.

The sound of the wind grew louder, and swirls of dust rose from the ground. I saw the creature ahead of me clearly, something large, and black, four-footed, with a long tail, more feline than canine; its eyes glowed.

"Who are you?" I cried out. "Why have you come here?"

It answered me with a snarl, then reared up to stand on its hind legs and take the shape of a man—

if such a creature could be called a man—wearing an animal's face and skin. It held a whip in its right hand.

I still grasped the banner of the Union in my left hand; now in my right hand I held a sword, with a gilded basket hilt and a blade that glittered as if it held lightning.

The first stroke of the creature's whip wrapped around the staff I held and jerked it from my grasp. The banner fell to the dusty earth.

The creature laid back its ears and snarled. The whip lashed out, cutting my arm. I ran, circling the beast, and the beast turned, running, to circle me. I struck with my sword, and cut only air.

Still we ran and turned, ran and turned, always in a leftward spiral, accomplishing nothing. I resolved to break the pattern. I would do two things: I would pluck the starry banner from the dust, and turn back onto a rightward path—deosil not widdershins, as the savants would have it said. All I thought was that whatsoever the creature wished me to do, and whithersoever the creature wished me to go, I would oppose.

Neither deed would be easy. Turning back rightward meant exposing myself to the whip. Taking up the banner would slow my progress, make me clumsy. I would not let these things dismay me.

Before I could act, the creature spoke.

"Woman," it said, its voice mellifluous. "Join me."

I cut right with the sword. The creature was too far away to strike, so that I had to stop and half turn to make my swing. The move slowed me.

"We are alike, we two," the creature said. "We should not fight."

I knew that it lied—even before the lash of its whip curled out and laid a line of fire across my back, I knew that it lied. There was the flag, lying in the dust. I took it up once more in my left hand.

"We are nothing alike," I said.

The lash wrapped around my right wrist, and jerked back. The beast was trying to disarm me.

"You control a spirit," it said. "As do I. When we combine them—"

"I control no spirits," I said. "What is in me is freely shared and freely given." The words vibrated in the air after I had spoken them, and I was inspired in turn—the wind spoke truth into my ears, and I uttered it.

"I name you William Walker," I said. "I command you. I conjure you. I demand you desist."

"Shall I try to guess *your* name?" it answered with a laugh, strange in that uncanny mouth, fanged and lipless. Its yellow eyes glowed. "Be my ally, not my enemy."

The wind was high now, blowing dust up into my eyes.

"Silence, traitor," I said. "I have Vanderbilt's commission for thy head. Liberty herself is my mistress, not thee."

The creature snarled and leapt at me, abandoning its lash. I dropped to my right knee and braced up the sword. The creature fell upon me; I wedged the sword against my lower leg and allowed the creature

to plunge downward upon its point. The beast
gnashed and rent the air with fangs and claws, strain-
ing to end me even as the sword protruded from its
back, and the dying creature's heavy weight dragged
the sword out of my hand.

Then the desert wilderness dissolved around me,
and I was in a drawing room, some place where the
air was sweet with flowers and a slave woman was
pouring me a cup of tea. Across the table from me sat
a short man with a high forehead, slender and clean-
shaven.

"Whom do I have the honor of addressing?" he
asked.

"One who loves liberty," I replied.

"You have come to my domain," he said. "I have far
more power than you; I can easily destroy you. Only
your beauty prevents the greatest of misfortunes
from befalling you."

"If you had that power," I said, "you would not be
sitting here talking."

The teacup in my hand became a sword, and I
struck him with it. He split in half; the room split in
half; and I was once again on the barren plain, with
the banner of liberty firm in my grip. Rain was falling, turning the dust to mud. Flickers of flame arose
from the earth only to be smothered by the rain.

I planted the flagstaff in the mud, and saw the banner lift and stir in the rising breeze. I raised the
sword over my head.

A bolt of lightning descended; my vision cleared;
and I was on the deck of *Nicodemus*, naked as I came

into this world and as I went for a while out of it, standing in my accustomed brass circle with empty hands.

The dark lines of whip strokes burned on my arm, on my wrist, and across my back. As the sunlight and the warm air touched them, they faded away.

*The narrative of Lieutenant
John Nevis, USN, continued.*

THE WORLD OPENED UP AGAIN AROUND US IN A dazzle of light. Moist, sun-warmed air enwrapped us, a gentle benison after the alternating clammy fog and arid chill of the far southern latitudes where we had lately sailed. I opened my eyes to a ship and a crew whole and undamaged, afloat on a tropic ocean. *Alecto* stood a cable-length away, not moving, with no man visible at gun or wheel or mast.

"*Nicodemus*, lay us alongside," I said. The ship did not hesitate, but smoothly obeyed. When our outboard strakes touched those of *Alecto* I said, "Away boarders." The boatswain piped; the men leapt over the side, myself at their head.

No living man remained on the Rebel's deck, and no one dead. The boards were frosted with rime that was fast vanishing in the hot sun; low fog rolled over the sides as it melted.

"She has a foul smell on her," said Mr. Bash. "Like a slaughterhouse."

I recalled that Mr. Bash had not been privy to the reports that Columbia and I had seen during our visit to London. "With good reason," I said. "Froggie and Captain Sharps together were a lightsome thing, next to what *Alecto* was."

" 'Was?' "

"I dare to hope so. I think the passage through the maelstrom cleansed it. Of metaphysical presences, at least." I strove not to breathe too deeply of the tainted air. "I don't think all the holystone and sand in the Navy could get rid of the smell."

"No, sir," said Mr. Bash.

"We'll have to look below anyway," I said. "There's no help for it."

The charnel-house reek grew even stronger as we descended, but the first spaces we entered below decks proved to be as deserted as above. I found the logbook in what I took to be the captain's cabin aft. I read a page, and closed it, my mind reeling from the blasphemy it revealed. Savants in Washington might want to see it; they could have it. I wanted to read nothing further.

Then we took lanterns and went farther down, into *Alecto*'s bilges, where the air was almost too foul and thick to breathe. There, as I had both feared and hoped, we found a number of wretches chained hand and foot to staples let into the timber of the ship's ribs. Most were short, swarthy men, but one was white, and he hailed me in English.

He was, as I had suspected, the last surviving member of the crew of the *Lucy Wainwright*; and he confirmed that the crew members taken off that unfortunate ship had been brought aboard *Alecto,* there to perish one by one to feed the hellish vessel's unceasing hunger.

"These other fellows mostly came later," he said. "I think the Rebels bought 'em somewhere. Brazil, maybe; one of 'em spoke a sort of Portuguese."

"We will strive to return them all home," I said. "But it may take some time. We have yet to make our own way back to port."

I directed Mr. Bash and the boarding party to free all the prisoners and convey them across to *Nicodemus,* where they could be washed and fed and exposed to sunshine and clean air. While these orders were being carried out, I returned to *Nicodemus* alone, the better to confer with my bride about *Alecto's* fate.

"Whatever inhabited her before," I said, "I think it's gone. But I can't see a ship like that one ever being lucky, no matter whether she goes by sail or steam."

"No," agreed Columbia. She stood on the deck of *Nicodemus* dressed in a gown of summery cotton. Such were the strange workings of the human mind, that those same rough sailors who had ceased to marvel when she paced the deck clad only as Eve had been in Eden, now could scarce look away. "The motive spirit may be gone, but the soul of the ship itself cannot have escaped corruption. Some part of it, I think, will always be hungry."

With the demise of Captain Sharps, my bride was

the most knowledgeable person aboard where matters metaphysical were concerned, and in this case, her fears and opinions marched with my own. I gave orders accordingly, and soon had the boatswain and his mates standing by.

"Are all of the former captives safe aboard *Nicodemus*?" I asked him, and upon obtaining an answer in the affirmative—"Take a sledgehammer and break her bell. Then burn the Rebel. Do it as safely as may be—I don't want a stray spark or careless flame to be the death of two ships instead of one— but see to it."

"Aye aye, sir," he said, and so it was done.

I, meanwhile, had other problems. We were alone in the wide sea, with no clue where we were, and with neither compass nor sextant nor chronometer to give us aid. Mr. Bash had suggested taking the instruments of navigation from *Alecto*, but I would trust nothing with that ship's taint on it aboard mine. Instead, I had determined to wait for sunset, locate the north star, and sail to latitude thirty north, then either east or west (it did not matter much to me which) until we found land.

Then a happy thought came to me, and I said, "*Nicodemus*, if you have not left us, please take us to New York." And with hardly felt acceleration we turned, put the sun on our beam, and headed northward.

*The narrative of Lieutenant
John Nevis, USN, concluded.*

OF THE CRUISE OF USS *NICODEMUS*, THERE IS
not much more to tell. We made good time on our
journey home to New York, the kind offices of the
freed spirit bringing us to within sight of the Sandy
Hook lightship inside twenty-three days—in no wise
the equal of our reckless pursuit of *Alecto* from the
equatorial regions through the Roaring Forties to the
far south Atlantic, but easily a match for the fastest
California clipper. At that time we broke out in earnest the sails which we had previously rigged as a
disguise in Portsmouth and in the Azores, and made
ready to bid farewell to the spirit of *Nicodemus*.

We had previously gathered together such metal
as could be spared; the brass ring on the deck in
which Miss Abrams had stood; hatchets, spikes,
and knives; and over a charcoal fire in the galley's
sandbox we had melted it, and therewith cast a bell.
This was hung just forward of the mizzen from a
frame erected for the purpose.

At noon on the fourteenth of July, just as the sun was making meridian passage to the south, and just as the Sandy Hook lightship hove into view above the horizon, I mustered the crew at quarters, in their dress uniforms. Eight sideboys stood to attention on the quarterdeck, the boatswain piped the side, and I struck the bell eight times and cried out, *"Nicodemus,* departing."

Down dropped the sails. Then came a fresh breeze from the port quarter, the sails bellied again, and we continued to make way (at a much slower rate) toward port.

"Did you feel it leaving?" Columbia asked.

"I did," said I, for I had indeed perceived a change to the ship; the air; the sea. So too, apparently, did the men, for they looked all about them in confusion.

The boatswain broke the silence. "Turn to, you laggards!" he cried. "We're sailormen now, and have sails to trim. Jump to it and lively!"

With that reassuring return of Naval activity, the crew commenced to perform their tasks as they would on any other ship. Its inhabiting spirit gone, *Nicodemus* was but an ordinary warship: a handy sailer, and no bad vessel to have as one's first command, but no longer the thing of fear and wonder that had come down the icy ways of Thule.

We came thus to Ambrose Channel, and followed the buoys to the Narrows and the Spider. There we raised signal for a tug, and were warped into Brooklyn Navy Yard.

As we entered the harbor, I glanced over at my old office on Whitehall Street. Less than a year had passed since last I gazed from those windows out over the harbor, hoping for a ship; yet here I was with my own command (however briefly) and a wife. Wonders, I thought, would never cease.

The brig *Triumph*, with Uncle Joe Suffern still in command, was in port at the time of our arrival, and before too many hours had passed Columbia and I were seated in his cabin, drinking coffee and exchanging tales of our adventures for news of the war.

We were heartened to learn the news of General Meade's victory at Gettysburg, and even more gratified—for my part, at least—to hear that the fortress of Vicksburg and the entirety of the Mississippi River were now in Union hands, after a campaign in which the Navy, under Rear-Admiral Porter, had played a vital part. Nor were we surprised to learn that newspapers in New York and in Richmond were reporting the recent unexpected death of President Walker of Nicaragua; he had collapsed, according to the *Times*, on Midsummer's Day of a sudden apoplexy.

"Mr. Vanderbilt," observed my wife upon hearing the story, "is not a man whom it pays to cross."

She and I, in our turn, regaled Captain Suffern with those of *Nicodemus*'s adventures which could be spoken of, and which were not private to ourselves alone.

"Burned her, you say?" he said when I had finished. "There's one or two metaphysical types in Washington who aren't going to be well pleased with you about that. They've been wanting to take a look at her."

"Sir," I said, "I would not have put my worst enemy aboard that ship, far less any seaman under my command."

"I expect the Navy will agree with you," Uncle Joe said equably. "There might even be a promotion in it for you, in the end."

"I would not have anyone think that I did my duty only for the sake of advancement," I said.

Columbia smiled at me. "No one will think that, John. They will think you are loyal and heroic and clever, and entirely deserving."

I blushed to hear her flatter me thus; but Uncle Joe only laughed and said that I was a lucky man to have so clever a wife. "Listen to what she tells you, my lad, and you'll never run aground."

The advice, I thought, was sound, and borne out by my own experiences. I determined at once to follow it, and have never had cause to regret the decision. I did in fact obtain my promotion, to lieutenant commander and a billet as first officer on USS *Ranger*; the other officers and men aboard *Nicodemus* likewise went to good billets. Columbia returned to Washington to live with her father until the end of the war, after which she and I made our home in Philadelphia with our own small family— which by that time had seen the arrival of a healthy daughter and, within a year of the Rebel surrender

at Appomattox, a son. *Nicodemus* herself was christened and recommissioned as USS *Conshohocken*,
and under that name serves honorably in the fleet
to this day.

Of the men who had sailed aboard CSS *Alecto*,
and descended with her into the maelstrom, none,
save the rescued prisoners, were ever seen again.

Authors' Note: William Walker

THE HISTORICAL WILLIAM WALKER (1824–1860) was equal in contemporary notoriety to his counterpart in this novel, though his successes were even more ephemeral. Born in Nashville, Tennessee, he graduated summa cum laude at fourteen from the University of Nashville, then studied medicine at the universities of Edinburgh in Scotland and Heidelberg in Germany before taking a degree in medicine from the University of Pennsylvania at age nineteen. Not content with a medical degree, he relocated to New Orleans, first to study, then practice law and edit the *New Orleans Crescent* newspaper. In 1849, the call of adventure, or perhaps of gold, brought him to San Francisco, where he practiced journalism, fought duels, and eventually conceived the first of his many plans to establish a white, English-speaking state in some part of Latin America.

In 1853, he set out with forty-five men in an attempt to conquer the Mexican territories of Sonora and Baja California. Despite his capture of the city of La Paz and his declaration of a new Republic of Lower California (with himself as president), he was in short order forced by the Mexican government to retreat back to California, where he was tried for conducting an illegal war. Filibustering, as such campaigns were known, was popular enough at the time that the jury took only eight minutes to acquit him.

In 1855, Walker tried his state-building tactics again, this time in Nicaragua, where the rebel faction in an ongoing civil war had hired him as a mercenary. He left San Francisco on May 4, 1855, with fifty-seven men (augmented upon his landing in Nicaragua with 170 locals and about a hundred additional U.S. citizens). Within six months he had defeated the Nicaraguan national army and taken control of the country through the establishment of a puppet regime under President Patricio Rivas. In 1856, U.S. president Franklin Pierce recognized Walker's regime as the legitimate government of Nicaragua. Finally, in July 1856, Walker declared himself president of Nicaragua after an uncontested election. At that time—possibly with an eye toward drawing increased support from southerners in the United States—he also revoked Nicaragua's emancipation edict of 1824, which had made slavery illegal.

Not content with these accomplishments, Walker began recruiting Americans and Europeans to come and fight for the conquest of the Central American nations of Guatemala, El Salvador, Honduras, and Costa Rica. By this time he was engaged in the feud with Cornelius Vanderbilt, which—in the real world as in the world of the novel—contributed to his ultimate downfall. Walker's revocation of the charter for Vanderbilt's Accessory Transit Company, and Vanderbilt's betrayal by his associates Charles Morgan and Cornelius K. Garrison, took place as related in the novel, as did Vanderbilt's promised and successful financial ruination of the pair.

. Vanderbilt continued his retaliation by pressuring the U.S. government to withdraw its recognition of Walker's regime. He also helped finance and provide training for a Costa Rican-led military coalition of the Central American states threatened by Walker. On May 1, 1857, under pressure by the Vanderbilt-financed Central American coalition and with his army reduced by cholera and desertion, Walker surrendered to Commander Charles H. Davis of the United States Navy and was sent back home to New Orleans.

Nothing daunted, within six months Walker set off again for Nicaragua, only to be arrested by the U.S. Navy Home Squadron and sent back to the United States for a second time. Walker then took a year off to write a book (*War in Nicaragua*, published in 1860), before heading back to Central America for a third try.

This time Walker was captured by the British

Royal Navy. The Royal Navy, rather than sending Walker home to plan yet another filibustering campaign, handed him over to the Honduran authorities. The Hondurans, out of patience with Walker's attempts at Central American empire-building, executed him by firing squad on September 12, 1860. He was thirty-six years old.